KU-077-407

Moving On

Ellie Langley swung herself out of her car in one elegant movement and then gazed across the bay to see if Beachy Head was in its usual place. It was of course, but she liked to make sure. Nearer at hand the white walls of the Culmore Pavilion were gleaming in the evening sunshine and looked beautiful against the background of sea and sky. A perfect day to wish her beloved father and his new bride a happy future together.

She reached over into the back seat of her Fiat for the bouquet she had placed there two hours before. Her new step-mother had been kind, sorry that Ellie's own relationship had foundered and hoping that the lovely roses and stephanotis would comfort her a little. And then Ellie's smiling father had come towards her with outstretched arms for a farewell hug.

'My beautiful daughter!' he murmured. 'Don't forget, Ellie, my love, that your home is always here if you need it.' She hugged him back.

'I know, Dad, and thanks.'

He had understood her need to get away from home and that the job she had been offered in Cheselton-on-Sea a couple of months ago was interesting enough to provide new challenges for her.

1

And now here she was, back again ready to take up the reins and to banish memories of Cheating Charles to the deepest recesses of her mind, never to think of him again. She hoped.

Smiling, she closed the garden gate behind her and paused to listen to the music floating from an open top floor window of the apartments. Vivaldi's *Four Seasons*? Her employer never tired of listening to this now she was virtually housebound. Ellie removed her sandals and glided barefoot across the freshly mown grass to the corner where her guinea pigs lived.

'You wouldn't like these flowers to eat,' she assured them as they came snuffle-nosed to the wire door to greet her. 'I'll find something much nicer for you, my pretty dears.'

No answer, of course, but she knew them too well to expect one.

She placed the bouquet on top of the hutch and then opened the door to lift out her two pets, holding their warm bodies close to her face for comfort and crooning softly to them.

'Amanda aimed her bridal flowers at me and I caught them without meaning to,' she murmured.

She gazed down at them and tried to suppress her unease about Dad's happiness. Amanda, ten years his junior, was light years younger in reality and Ellie's heart ached for him with a suddenness that was painful.

A red admiral butterfly came fluttering and swooping above the spring flowers by the wall. Ellie began to sing, swaying gently from side to side. 'Love is wonderful for sure . .' and then, forgetting the words, hummed the catchy tune instead. Not brilliant, but Flora and Dinah raised no objections. She kissed their smooth heads and then began to dance, twisting and turning, the skirt of her colourful dress twirling round her.

As a baritone voice joined in Ellie stopped and swung round, startled. The man looking at her was tall and broad shouldered with a mass of wavy brown hair.

She felt colour flood her cheeks

'Who are you?' she said, embarrassed. 'What are you doing here?'

'I've come to see Miss Valence,' he said, his voice deep and musical.

'By creeping up on me and frightening me out of my wits?'

He smiled. 'You have a perfect pitch and a lovely tone in your voice. I had no means of knowing you were dancing with such abandon or I might have restrained myself. I apologise.'

'So you're a choir master?'

'Hardly that.'

'An opera singer, then?'

'No way.' When he smiled he became, all at once, devastating. 'As I said I'm a mere visitor calling on Miss Lola Valence. I believe that's allowed?'

3

She pretended to consider, a smile curving her lips.

'Of course,' she said 'But you should use the front entrance because the bells to the apartments are there. Ring the top one and Miss Valence will answer.'

'You seem very sure of that.'

'I should do. I work for her.'

'You do?' He sounded surprised.

'It's perfectly reasonable for her to have a secretary and general factotum now that using her hands is difficult.'

'Well, yes, of course. But do you often dance barefoot on the grass with two strange animals?'

'Guinea pigs,' Ellie said

'Guinea pigs,' he repeated, a gleam of amusement in his eyes.

She ignored his question and walked across the grass with the intention of retrieving her sandals. But she had forgotten her precious cargo still held protectively to her.

'Difficult to manage holding those, isn't it?' he said, following her. 'Here, let me.' He put out his right hand to take the guinea pigs from her.

She took a step back. 'In that suit?' she said

'What's wrong with my suit?'

She gazed at it critically . . . light grey and expensive-looking. Shirt pristine white and his tie blue and green in a swirly pattern that reminded her of the sea. He looked vulnerable

4

now as if her approval mattered.

'It's not bad,' she admitted. 'But it'll show every hair.'

His mouth twitched.

'So there's a special magic about that beautiful dress you're wearing that prevents their hairs coming off on you?'

Before she could say anything the violin music ceased. Ellie looked up and saw her employer at the window

'Is that my visitor, Eloise?' Miss Valence called down to her.

'Eloise?' he said 'A pretty name.'

She felt her cheeks grow warm again.

'Send him up at once, please.' The window slammed shut.

'Phew!' he said 'Do I swarm up the ivy and tap on the glass or what?' He looked down at his left hand, which was held limply at his side.

'Not in that suit.'

'Then the front entrance it will have to be,' he said

He had a presence that seemed to fill his surroundings with interest. Now that he had gone Ellie felt bereft and slightly foolish at being caught swirling around and singing about love to a couple of fluffy animals.

She put them back into their hutch then collected her sandals. Suitably shod, she then went into her ground floor apartment by the back door.

When she had answered Miss Valence's

5

advertisement some months ago, she found that accommodation in Bredon Court where she lived, was provided for the successful applicant so that all the help and support needed in her debilitating illness was always on hand. This turned out to be a beautifully furnished ground-floor flat with background colours of pearl and cream that set off the dark furniture. The multi-coloured rug that Dad had managed to bring back from one of his cycling trips to France gave the finishing touch.

To allow plenty of time for the visitor to depart Ellie changed out of her dress and hung it with care in her wardrobe. The sandals went in their box for safe keeping and the tiny feathery concoction that she had hoped wouldn't show much on her dark wavy hair went into another. The bouquet! Oh no, she had left Amanda's beautiful arrangement on top of the hutch.

Dressed now in jeans and T-shirt, she went through to the kitchen and out into the walled garden that belonged to her apartment. She was aware of how fortunate she was to have the use of it, not only for Flora and Dinah's sake, but also because she loved the feel of bare earth on her hands and the joy of growing things.

The violin music started up again, fainter now because the window was closed. This must mean that Miss Valence was alone and would expect her to report at once on the day's events.

Ignoring the lift, Ellie ran lightly up the flight of stairs to the first floor landing and tapped on her employer's door. Miss Valence was seated in her chair near the CD-player. The control was close to her on a small table and now she reached towards it and pressed a switch so that the music came to a stop once again. Ellie knew better than to offer to do it for her, but it was painful to watch the slow movements.

'For me?' Miss Valence said with pleasure as Ellie placed the bouquet in her lap. 'You're a kind girl, Ellie, my dear.'

Ellie pulled a chair forward and sat down. 'Did you miss me today?'

'Not a bit. Did you expect me to?'

Ellie laughed and shook her head. Her employer hated having to rely on others and made sure they realised this.

'So tell me all about your father's wedding,' Miss Valence said.

Ellie began by describing the flowers in the church and Amanda's lacy cream dress. She told her how the smallest bridesmaid, overawed, had tripped as the bridal party came down the aisle. Dad had turned just in time to catch her and carry her out giggling into the sunshine with them.

What she didn't say, in case it evoked painful memories in her employer of her own

7

piano-playing days, was that Amanda's cousin had played piano music at the reception so beautifully, that it had brought tears to Elle's eyes.

Miss Valence sighed. 'Your father must have been so proud.'

'Oh, he was,' said Ellie, thinking of Dad's shining eyes as he gazed down at his bride. Dear Dad. He deserved to be happy.

She made tea for them both, removed the bouquet and placed a glass dish of Miss Valence's favourite shortbread biscuits close to her.

'You're reliable and trustworthy, Ellie, and a hard worker,' Miss Valence said 'I hope you know how much I appreciate you But now I've a favour to ask and I don't like doing it You were talking to my last visitor?'

Ellie felt her cheeks glow as she poured the tea and placed her employer's cup and saucer on the table at her side. Since the man Miss Valence alluded to had left her standing in the garden he had filled her thoughts more than she liked. She wished she could ask who he was but somehow the words wouldn't come.

'Don't look so surprised, my dear. I must say I thought highly of him. People have been in and out all day. There's been so much to discuss. You see, there's been a crisis.'

'A crisis?'

'The festival organiser has pulled out suddenly.'

8

'He has? But that's terrible.'

For months the Culmore Pavilion had been undergoing renovation. This was now almost complete and the music festival in August was in celebration of this. For the organiser to pull out now would be catastrophic. Because of past family connections Miss Valence was heavily involved in the arrangements. Take that away from her and she would feel that her life might well be over.

Miss Valence gave a little shrug. 'You see the problem?'

'But why?'

'Family illness, I understand.'

'But can you find someone else at such short notice?'

Miss Valence moved her fingers backwards and forwards on the arms of her chair.

'Someone between jobs,' she said 'We're lucky to be able to take up my great-niece's suggestion, but I'm not at liberty to say much about it at the moment.'

Ellie felt a flicker of relief. 'I see. So what happens now?'

'You're a good girl, Ellie, and I don't want you to take this amiss.' Miss Valence cleared her throat and hesitated. Then, rubbing her swollen hand against her face she said quietly, 'Just this my dear. I have no choice but to ask you to vacate your apartment for a few weeks.'

Taken aback, Ellie looked at her in silence.

'My great-niece, Marsha, is anxious to

stay here with me and she needs to be on the ground floor.'

'But why . . .' Ellie broke off, unable to hide the hurt in her voice.

Miss Valence leaned forward and patted Ellie's hand. Her eyes shone with warmth.

'No-one else could look after me at as well as you do, my dear, and that won't change.'

Ellie bit her lip. 'But where will I live to be close enough to you if you need help?'

Miss Valence frowned. 'I can't turn my tenants out.'

'Of course not' Ellie knew only too well that they were all elderly and often needed attention that she had been only too pleased to give.

'Marsha's family, you see.' Miss Valence's, voice trembled lightly. 'Although, sadly, I haven't seen much of her since she moved to London. She was such a pretty little thing when she was growing up and I was fond of her.'

The cup rattled in the saucer as Miss Valence reached for her tea and took a sip. Then she gazed down at the cup in her hand as if she was wondering what it was doing there.

'Marsha has agreed to organise an art exhibition at the Culmore Pavilion at the same time as the music festival,' she said.

'I see,' Ellie said as she took the cup from her before the contents spilt.

Miss Valence looked sad.

'No, I don't think you do, Ellie. Marsha had a bad accident some weeks ago and broke her ankle. I've only just learnt that and I was rather surprised.'

'But how can she run an art exhibition with a broken ankle?'

'That's where you come in, my dear. I'd like you to give Marsha all the assistance you can.'

'But I don't know anything about artists and art festivals.'

'All you'll have to do is help Marsha pull it all together. Your computer skills will be invaluable.'

'But where will I live?'

'Ah yes, I was coming to that.' Miss Valence looked anxious. She moved a little in her chair, reached out for her cup and saucer again but then thought better of it.

'There are rooms in the loft that can be cleared out,' said Miss Valence. 'They've been used as store rooms for a long time and there's a bathroom on the floor below. If we put a bed in and an easy chair that would be adequate for a short while, don't you think? Your office will remain where it, is in the ground floor apartment as its just one small room with the computer and book shelves. Marsha won't mind that.'

'I see,' Ellie said again, willing herself not to show by her reaction that she felt deeply concerned. There would be no connecting bell to her employer's apartment in case of

11

emergencies and her mobile couldn't pick up a signal at Bredon Court.

Miss Valence leaned forward. 'You'll agree to this for my sake, Eloise? I shall be so glad to see more of Marsha.'

Ellie nodded, hiding her anxiety beneath a bright smile.

'I Like A Challenge'

Adam Merville emerged from the front entrance of Bredon Court and paused to look across the road at the Culmore Pavilion. The late sunshine muted the glaring white of the building to a subtle shade of pinkish cream. Even the traffic noise had subsided a little now. He took a deep breath of salty air then strode across to take a closer look at the place that was likely to demand his full attention for the best part of the coming two months if the position of the Culmore Music Festival Organiser became his.

'We need someone to front the preparations for the forthcoming festival that have been done so far,' Miss Valence had said 'Temporary, of course. And a figurehead.' Her eyes had bored through him as if daring him to query her words.

Figurehead, indeed! Any fool would know that taking on this job was anything but that.

12

The festival committee who had interviewed him had made that clear. They had also told him that a permanent overall manager for the Culmore was being sought and several applications had been received already.

He nodded. 'I like a challenge.'

She beamed approval. He could see that she must have been beautiful once. She was talented, too, if all he had heard was true. It was a cruel fate that had crippled her hands and cut short her career as a concert pianist.

In his own case he'd allowed his quick temper to overcome his common sense when dealing with a jeering thug outside the concert hall in Leeds. To his shame he had lashed out at him and injured his hand. He was lucky that this wasn't the end of his musical. ambitions.

'Well done, young man. You won't regret it.'

Unseen by her he flexed his left hand, testing the muscles in case by some miracle they had regained their strength. But no, not yet. A month or two more and hopefully he'd be back touring with the Cellini Orchestra once again.

Miss Valence straightened in her chair, her eyes full of purpose, a fighter if ever there was one. But strangely this very quality gave her a vulnerability in her present circumstances that was touching. Suddenly he found he wanted to please her.

'I'll be prepared to fill the position to the

13

best of my ability if they'll have me,' he said.

She nodded. 'Very good.'

He thought suddenly of the girl he had met in the garden who obviously had her employer's welfare at heart. There must be a soft centre somewhere in this powerful-seeming person to inspire her loyalty.

She nodded in dismissal. 'Thank you.'

With the keys Miss Valence had lent him, he unlocked the narrow door at the side of the pavilion's main entrance and went inside, locking it behind him. The deserted foyer smelled of paint and new furnishings. A pleasant sort of smell in the circumstances, showing that the work on the interior was almost complete. Not long now until the place was up and running.

Ignoring the rooms on either side, he headed for the balcony and unlocked one of the glass doors that gave access to it.

The view was magnificent. He spotted an abandoned chair and sat down, stretched out his legs and gazed at the expanse of greyish blue sea, glinting silver in places as if someone had illuminated it from below.

At last his fortunes appeared to be changing with the prospect of this temporary job in a pleasant place where he could begin to get his life back together again. He thought of the elderly Miss Valence seated in her beautiful apartment with her arthritic hands held loosely in her lap and knew how lucky he was in meeting her young relative when he had. When the old lady had talked of her great-niece her lined face had lit up and she had admitted that it was her plan to get her involved in the festival and she hoped that they would work well together. He had caught a brief glimmer of speculation in her eyes that gave him a momentary pause, but he had been glad enough to agree.

He'd been sitting there for only a few minutes when his solitude was disturbed by the sound of voices. Leaping to his feet, he leaned over the balustrade. No one down below. Inside then. Youngsters with nothing better to do fooling around, most likely. But they shouldn't have been able to get inside the building.

Perturbed now, he left the balcony. The foyer was deserted but there was a faint whiff of musky perfume lingering near the door now into what was obviously the retail outlet for pavilion memorabilia. It reminded him of Marsha, but no way could Marsha be here now. And neither should anyone else. His first concern, if his appointment was confirmed, would be to check why an efficient burglar alarm system wasn't already in operation. A black mark for somebody.

As he was about to go out of the building he noticed two women walking away, heading slowly for the lone car in the car park. They paused at the vehicle, deep in conversation.

He waited until they got in at last and had driven away.

He had blamed youngsters breaking into the place where they had no reason to be, but how unfair was that? For some reason he had become too quick to jump to the wrong conclusions since his accident. He would have to watch that.

If he came to work here . . . when, he corrected himself, his long-held dream of passing on his love of music to the younger generation might become a possibility. The new manager, of course, would have the most say. For a moment he allowed himself to wonder how he would feel if he were the successful applicant.

Smiling, he set off along the seafront to the Avalon Hotel where he was spending the next few nights until the flat allocated to him at the Culmore Pavilion was ready for occupation.

* * *

Ellie was up early next morning ready for her first job of the day. Taking the dog, Daisy, for her walk was a pleasure, not a duty, especially on a beautiful morning like this with the haze lifting from the horizon and sunshine breaking through in a golden path across the sea.

With the sun full on her face Ellie stepped out briskly along the seafront in the crisp air. Sunlight touched the metal masts of the sailing

16

dinghies lined up near their clubhouse. The tide was out and the exposed rocks gleamed in the sunshine, standing out from the wet sand like stranded sea creatures among the rock pools.

Ellie jumped down on to the beach with a clatter of disturbed pebbles and ran across with Daisy to reach the wet sand beyond. Releasing the dog, she watched her canter off in the joy of being free. She followed, avoiding the puddles of shining water that the outgoing sea had left behind.

After a while Ellie let out a piercing whistle that was her signal to Daisy to come back at once. In the distance the dog stopped, raised her head and then set off towards her at high speed, deflected only when she caught sight of a couple of gulls at the water's edge.

'I'd be doing just the same if I were a dog,' a voice said from behind her.

Ellie swung round. She didn't know how she hadn't heard his approach and felt at a disadvantage.

'Are you following me?' she said.

He was dressed casually today in jeans and green sweatshirt.

'I'm exploring my new territory,' he said pleasantly.

'This is your territory?' she asked with interest. There was something about him that inspired confidence so that if he told her that he owned it all she would have had no

17

difficulty in believing him.

'So to speak.'

'And how's that?'

'You're thinking I'm a smuggler or a coastguard perhaps? Or maybe a Punch and Judy man sussing out a good pitch?'

'It's too early in the year for that,' she said, smiling.

The lines round his eyes deepened as he smiled, too.

'Is the dog yours?'

'She belongs to one of our tenants, Mrs Drew.'

She looked across to where she had last seen Daisy and let out another piercing whistle.

'My,' he said in admiration. 'I wish I could do that.'

This time Daisy came streaming back and Ellie attached the lead, murmuring words of praise.

He bent to pat the dog's brindled body and Daisy squirmed in pleasure.

'Another of your jobs?' he asked.

'A voluntary one.'

'You're a girl of many parts. Miss Valence spoke highly of you.'

'She did?' Ellie looked at him suspiciously.

'Does that surprise you?'

She shrugged. 'She's very kind.'

'But not blinded by kindness to be certain of your value.'

18

Ellie felt herself flush at his intent gaze.

He glanced away and then back again.

'If all goes well I'll be working at the Culmore,' he said 'And, no before you ask, not as the janitor or in charge of catering.'

She giggled. He looked so boyish standing there with the sun behind his head that suddenly she could see what he'd been like as a little boy . . . a sensitive face, anxious grey eyes and a smudge of dirt on the sleeve of his shirt.

She blinked herself back into the present moment.

'The new organiser of the music festival?' she said. 'Are congratulations in order or should I be commiserating?'

'The music and art festival,' he corrected. 'My appointment should be confirmed today and then congratulations would be appreciated.'

They began to walk back across the beach. When they reached the pebbles he put out a hand to steady her when she nearly lost her balance as Daisy tried to surge ahead.

Immediately Ellie pulled free and then was ashamed of her quick reaction. She flushed again.

'Thank you,' she said

*   *   *

Ellie felt immersed in choking dust and

19

cobwebs as she and Ginette made a start on clearing the contents of the loft.

Her fellow worker looked anything but pleased about the task in hand. Ginette Kent had been Miss Valence's cleaner for longer than she cared to remember. Or so she said But Ellie knew she was only a couple of years older than herself and liked to joke. She also knew that Ginette's passion in life was sailing and to fund this activity and give her the free time when she needed it the job was highly suitable. From the first they had become firm friends.

Ginette picked up a moth-eaten blanket, gave it a good shake and set the pair of them off coughing.

'Put that thing down,' Ellie said when she had regained her breath. 'What a dreary way to spend an afternoon.'

'I can think of a better way.'

'Me, too.'

'And all because of Wonder Girl coming and taking over.' Ginette grimaced. 'I can't think what's got in to her. Or rather I can, the little gold digger.'

'You can't say that,' Ellie said.

'Can't I just. Wait till you meet her.'

Ginette said this in such a heartfelt way that Ellie laughed. In the mood Ginette was in she wasn't going to risk asking what Marsha was really like. Instead she thought of the man she now knew as Adam Merville. She had asked

20

Miss Valence about him on her return from walking Daisy.

'He's a good musician himself, as well as highly recommended,' her employer had said as she seated herself at the breakfast table. 'He's a saxophonist and piano player, freelancing at the moment because of a hand injury. Plenty of good contacts so he'll be useful to us.'

He seemed approachable, too, Ellie thought, and that was a good quality in the person in charge. Now, busy heaving heavy dusty boxes about, her mind dwelt on Adam Merville with pleasure.

Ginette tugged at a box and overbalanced, landing in a heap on the floor. Laughing, she got to her feet, brushing dust and cobwebs from her denim cut-offs.

'That's better,' Ellie said 'I was beginning to wonder what I'd done wrong.'

'Not you for sure,' Ginette said. 'That horrible madam, Marsha. She never comes near Miss Valence and now here she is turning you out of your apartment on a mere whim.'

Ellie sat back on her heels and brushed her damp hair away from her face.

'Not a whim, Ginette. She is organising an art exhibition as part of the festival.'

Ginette gave a scornful laugh. 'Art exhibition!'

'Someone has to do it.'

'What person in their right mind decides

21

to organise something like that when she's broken her ankle?'

'Someone like Marsha, full of determination?'

'If you say so.'

Ellie leapt to her feet.

'Let's get on with it. Things may not be as bad as we think.'

'Don't you believe it,' Ginette said with feeling. 'They're going to be a great deal worse.'

* * *

Ellie clicked open a file on her computer, ready to make a start on some lists her employer needed in preparation for the opening ceremony. In her imagination she felt the cheerfulness in the air on that special day and saw sunshine sparkling the sea. The Culmore Pavilion would once again be at the centre of a revival of local pride just as it had been when Miss Valence's grandfather was involved with the building all those years ago.

After a while she got up and went across to the window and looked down on the back garden. Ginette was out there now with the lawnmower, preparing to cut the lawn for her. She looked up and waved. For a moment Ellie wished she was out there with her, scooping up some of the cut grass for her guinea pigs and having a laugh about something or other as

22

they often did when they got together.

Back at her desk again, Ellie heard the roar of the machine start up and smiled to herself All at once her own task seemed easier.

The front door bell rang.

'A bumper crop today,' the postman said, grinning. 'Birthday?'

'I wish,' she said, taking the pile of correspondence from him.

No prizes for guessing what it was, she thought as she ran lightly up the stairs and tapped on her employer's door.

Miss Valence was seated in her usual high-backed chair by the window. Ellie pulled a chair forward and slit open the envelopes for her.

Miss Valence pulled out the first letter.

'As I thought,' she said with satisfaction. 'A request for the application forms for the art exhibition.'

'That's good,' Ellie said, taking it from her. 'I expect the others will be all the same. We've had several by e-mail, too. I'll see to them all now, shall I?'

'After the festival committee meeting over the road,' Miss Valence said firmly. 'But we'll have our coffee first.'

Ellie smiled. 'Coffee it is, then.'

Several others were there before them when they arrived at the committee room at the Culmore Pavilion. Miss Valence seated herself comfortably, Ellie at her side, when a stir in the doorway announced the arrival of Adam Merville.

He came in briskly, looking round to check who was present and bowing slightly in the direction of Miss Valence.

'The secretary?' he asked as he seated himself at the head of the table.

'Ellie's here to take the minutes,' Miss Valence said. He frowned. 'Is there no official secretary?'

'Until she's back from holiday Eloise is as official as anyone can possibly be,' Miss Valence said with some asperity. 'What's wrong with her I'd like to know?'

He cleared his throat.

'My mistake, Eloise. I apologise. Then let's get on with the proceedings, shall we?'

Ellie kept her eyes down on her pad as the meeting progressed. In spite of his conciliatory words Miss Valence's retort seemed to hang in the air and made her feel uncomfortable. She resolved to do an expert job to prove that she could be as professional as anybody in case he had any lingering doubts as to her ability.

Meeting Marsha

Afterwards Adam came across to her. 'Sorry about that at the beginning,' he said 'Put it down to nerves on my part.'

'Nerves?' Miss Valence said. 'Don't give me that young man.'

He smiled at Ellie. 'I could see I embarrassed you Now how shall I make it up to you? Are you free for a little while?'

'She has notes to type up and circulate,' Miss Valence said, a sharpness in her voice that surprised Ellie.

He shrugged. 'I hoped she might care to show me round town and perhaps have a bite to eat afterwards?'

Miss Valence's expression was icy.

'Eloise has plenty else to do as well as the minutes. No time to waste.'

He looked alarmed. Did he imagine her employer kept such a sharp rein on her that she was little better than a slave, Ellie wondered. It wasn't like that at all, of course. Miss Valence was kindness itself and must have realised how much she would have liked to accept. There would be some good reason for her blunt words, but she couldn't at the moment imagine what it was.

She tried to smile.

'Perhaps some other time?'

He bowed slightly.

'Of course.'

Ginette had finished her grass-cutting now and outside there was silence as Ellie sat down at the computer once again and concentrated on getting the minutes of the committee meeting into some sort of shape. Then she carried the printout up to her employer's apartment.

Miss Valence put the typed sheets on her table without glancing at them.

'Is something wrong?' Ellie asked.

'I need to explain about the new festival organiser. I have to tell you, my dear, that he has additional commitments.'

Ellie flushed. 'You mean as well as the Culmore Pavilion and the music festival?'

'There is the question of his fiancée.'

'Fiancée?'

Miss Valence tapped her fingers on her chair.

'He should have been thinking of her instead of asking you to accompany him.'

'It was just a request to be shown something of the town,' Ellie said. 'Nothing more.'

'So it would seem, my dear. But it would not be wise in this case. Knowing her as I do I fear she would not be pleased.'

Ellie said nothing. Surely trust was the important thing here?

Miss Valence's chair creaked as she moved into a more comfortable position. 'I understand from Ginette that the rooms on the top floor are very nearly habitable?'

'Well, yes,' Ellie said, glad to have something else to think about. Ginette had found her a single bed and mattress from the basement. There was a chest of drawers as

26

well.

'When do you expect your great-niece to arrive?' she asked.

'Soon, I believe. Apparently Adam, her fiancé, was most insistent that she take up residence here as soon as possible. They have a lot to discuss.'

'Adam?' Ellie said. Adam, of course. Adam Merville, the new man at the Culmore. This was such an obvious explanation for Marsha wanting to come and stay here that she marvelled that something of the sort hadn't occurred to her before.

*　　*　　*

Daisy wriggled in excitement, uttered little cries of anticipation and then started off at a smart pace as if she knew that Ellie had planned a visit to the park this time. A gentle breeze stirred the branches of the trees and hazy sunlight reflected on the calm water of the lake.

Ellie walked slowly, allowing the warm sunshine to dispel the tension she was beginning to feel with her extra workload. Driving Miss Valence to her various appointments at the hospital, optician and dentist the following week would be time-consuming but Adam Merville and his fiancée, Marsha, would no doubt be working close together soon so that her assistance with the

27

art exhibition preparations wouldn't be quite so necessary.

She called Daisy and put the lead on. It was tempting to linger for a while in this peaceful place but there were things to do back at Bredon Court.

Just as she put her key into the lock on the front door a taxi drew up. The driver opened the passenger door. The occupant reached for a pair of crutches and began to lever herself out of the cab.

Ellie's heart leapt. Marsha arriving early! She rushed towards her

'Can I help?' she asked breathlessly.

The fragile-looking girl paused and looked at Ellie enquiringly.

'And you are?'

'I'm Ellie Langley, Miss Valence's P.A. You must be Marsha. 'Let me . . .'

But Marsha shrugged her off Ellie watched as she finished manoeuvring herself out of the vehicle while the taxi driver piled the luggage on the pavement.

'Inside the building, if you please,' Marsha ordered.

He hesitated and then picked up the two largest suitcases. Ellie held the door open for him as he staggered back and forth. Marsha saw to his payment, pulling the money from the pocket of her smart pink jacket.

'Show me where my apartment is and I'll get my belongings in,' she said to Ellie as the taxi

28

drove off.

'I can't let you do that,' Ellie said, appalled.

'Why not? It was the sort of welcome I was expecting.' Marsha looked around her large entrance hall and then back at Ellie. 'You wouldn't think I'm the old lady's only relative, would you?' She sounded condemning as if it was Miss Valence's fault.

Marsha was still gazing up at the building moments later when Ellie had returned Daisy to her owner.

'My great-aunt was decidedly doddery when I saw her last,' Marsha said 'I expect she's aged a lot since then.'

Ellie, busy lifting the suitcases inside, didn't answer. Surely she had imagined that hint of anticipation in Marsha's voice? But tiredness could account for her not realising just how that sounded.

Marsha frowned as gazed round the sitting-room.

'I'll make sure everything's just how you like it as soon as I can,' Ellie said.

'You'd better open the window and let some fresh air in then.'

Ellie did so. Then she took the crutches as Marsha seated herself in the arm chair and placed a footstool nearby.

'I don't like people fussing,' Marsha said 'I can manage.' She leaned forward and hoisted her plastered leg on to the stool with obvious difficulty.

29

Ellie hesitated. 'If you're sure you're all right for a minute or two I'll just use the phone in the office to let your great-aunt know that you're here.'

'Do what you will.' Marsha leaned back and closed her eyes, her hair shining in a golden halo against the crimson cushion.

Ellie noted the pallor of the girl's face and the dark shadows beneath her eyes. 'I'll be only a moment and then I'll put the kettle on,' she said.

'Don't bother,' Marsha whispered as if mouthing the words was an effort.

Ellie went to her office next door. Here everything was just the same as always and she felt a moment's relief to see her familiar desk with her PC and the bookshelves lining the walls.

She picked up the phone and clicked the button to connect her to her employer's apartment.

*   *   *

In her eyrie at the top of the house, Ellie eyed the jumble of boxes and suitcases strewn about the small room with dismay. If Marsha was critical of the apartment downstairs she would be disgusted at the state of this one.

Miss Valence's voice on the phone had trembled a little when she heard that her niece had arrived. Ellie had been quick to reassure her that everything was in order and that she would be up right away to escort her down in the lift.

Miss Valence's face had been flushed as she greeted Marsha. 'And have you everything you need, my dear?' she said 'I'm sure Ellie will help you with your unpacking?'

Ellie pulled up a chair for her.

'There's no need for that,' Marsha said. 'As soon as you're both gone I shall see to everything myself My fiancé is taking me to dinner at the Royal Hotel so you needn't worry that I'll be bothering you.'

The lines round Miss Valence's mouth deepened.

'So your young man knew exactly when you were coming?'

'Of course'

Miss Valence pursed her lips.

'I shall stay a few minutes longer, Ellie,' she said 'I shall manage the lift by myself.'

Ellie nodded and left them. She knew that Miss Valence would have welcomed a show of affection from Marsha and she felt hurt on her behalf that she hadn't got it.

When Ellie had done enough unpacking for the time being she glanced at her watch. Flora and Dinah would think she had neglected them if she didn't appear soon with their food.

Down in the garden she felt the energy trickle back into her as she tended to her pets. To her relief the surprising pain she had felt

31

at thinking of Adam and Marsha together was beginning to fade now. What sort of person was she to resent the happiness of others when Adam was nothing to her . . . decidedly selfish? An unattractive quality, especially in this case when Marsha was at such a disadvantage with her injured ankle.

Ellie took a deep breath, resolved to settle into her new accommodation and get on with life and be pleased that someone close to Miss Valence was happy and that she could help her with the job on band. It could be done and she would do it.

The garden gate crashed open.

'Hi there!' Ginette called in her throaty voice.

Ellie spun round as her friend appeared with her arms full of bulky cushions. She eyed their bright patterns of reds, oranges and purples with astonishment.

'These are for you,' Ginette gasped as one of them slid from her grasp. 'I rescued them from a pile of junk my mum was sorting for the charity shop.'

' "Junk"?' Ellie said faintly.

Ginette laughed. 'Only in a manner of speaking. These are the very best quality Feel them, Ellie. My gran made them years ago but somehow they got forgotten after she died and for some reason Mum hates them.'

Bemused, Ellie ran her fingers across the bright material, liking the feel of luxurious

32

softness as well as their bright colours.

'I thought they'd liven your place up,' Ginette said 'What do you think"

Ellie was cheered by her friend's kindness. 'Let's get them upstairs and see.'

Ginette burst into the loft apartment and shed her cargo on the floor. Ellie, following, dropped the cushion she was carrying on to the nearest chair and stood back to see the effect.

'Brilliant,' Ginette said in satisfaction. 'If you've got to be up here they're just the job. Mind you, I can't think why you can't move into the empty apartment on the second floor while the new tenant's still in New Zealand.'

Ellie shook her bead. 'That's not possible.' She picked up the three cushions and placed them on her bed. The vibrant splashes of colour brightened the gloom in a way that was definitely pleasing.

Ginette gazed at them with pride. 'See what I mean?' Ellie felt a lump in her throat at her friend's generosity and she swallowed hard.

'They're truly beautiful,' she said. 'Thanks, Ginette, you're a pal.'

'Think nothing of it' Are you still busy? I thought we'd go out somewhere to celebrate the arrival of Wonder Girl.'

'So you know she's arrived?'

'And how,' Ginette said with feeling. 'Come on then if you're coming.'

'But I thought tonight was race night at the sailing club?'

33

'There's a new place opened along the front. Fancy giving it a go?'

'Afterwards,' Ellie said firmly. 'I want to come and watch you sail first, but I'll just check on Miss Valence and see if she needs anything.'

Ginette looked pleased. 'You want to watch me sail? I never thought I'd live to hear you to say that.'

Ellie had surprised herself, too, when the words came out of her mouth. Until now she enjoyed hearing of her friend's exploits on the water but had never had an urge to watch her at close quarters. But after the hassle of Marsha's arrival she felt she needed to get away from Bredon Court for a while.

* * *

This was the first time Ellie had been inside the clubhouse and she looked round with interest at the bustling scene. The laughter and joking were cheering to someone who was feeling a little sidelined by recent events. She smiled as she moved through them to find a suitable chair on the balcony.

From here she had a good view of the proceedings as everyone began to get their boats ready for the race. She watched the rescue boat shoot out from the shore and head for the horizon. It slowed down as someone tipped something overboard and then it set off in a different direction to place buoys at intervals to mark the course for the dinghies.

The boats were on the water now, all jostling for position. The starting gun fired and they were off. At first it was hard to pick Ginette out among the other sailors but then Ellie recognised the number in large black figures on the white sail of her boat. Ginette was moving up a place each time she rounded a buoy until at last she came in just behind the leader as the race finished.

Ellie ran down to the beach to meet her and helped pull her boat to its accustomed place.

'Did you see that last lap?' Ginette said enthusiastically. 'I almost pulled it off and came in first. The new chap beat me to it at the last minute.'

She didn't seem at all put out Ellie noticed. In fact she looked positively jubilant.

When they had placed the cover on the boat and made sure it was secure Ellie went back to the clubroom to wait for her friend to change out of her sailing gear.

'It's great being out there on the water,' Ginette said as she joined her, her face still glowing and her eyes bright. 'There's nothing like it for forgetting your troubles. Fancy joining us, Ellie? You'd soon learn.'

Ellie laughed. 'With the festival coming up? You're joking.' But for the first time since she had known Ginette she could see the pleasure in it, the sense of achievement in battling with the elements, the feeling of freedom as you race through the waves.

'I'll ask you afterwards.' Ginette promised with a glint in her eye that told Ellie she wouldn't forget. 'I don't know about you, but I'm starving.'

They sat outside enjoying the fading sunlight while Beachy Head merged into a distant haze and the incoming tide rattled the pebbles on the beach. A few people passed, elderly mostly and obviously on their accustomed evening walks, with their dogs. Then came a group of younger ones with rucksacks and sailing bags.

'Hi, Ginette!' one of them called.

'Hi,' she responded, gazing at him, her face suffused with colour. She looked dreamily after him as he passed.

'So what's his name?' Ellie asked.

'He's a new chap, Sam Gerard, from Southampton, a brilliant sailor. Just landed himself a plum of a job at Hackett and Blunts. You know the printing firm in Mendaville Square?'

'He looks nice,' Ellie said. Sam was as tall and broad-shouldered as Adam but not a bit like him, fair-haired while Adam was dark, and a lot sturdier-looking. Adam had a pensive air about him, too, while Sam seemed to burst with physical energy.

Ginette nodded. 'Did you see him go round the last mark? He's been down in Cornwall for

36

the Southern Championships before he moved here. He's really lovely.'

Ellie smiled at her friend. 'I can see that you seem to know a lot about him already.'

'Oh well, we don't often have new people turning up.'

'Until the festival gets going.' Ellie sighed. She felt tired now and anxious to be back at Bredon Court. She hurriedly repressed a shimmer of envy as she thought of Marsha enjoying Adam's company.

'Wonder Girl still getting to you?' Ginette asked.

'She looks so frail and I'm not sure how she'll cope with organising the art exhibition.'

'Frail?' Ginette scoffed. 'She got herself here from London, didn't she? I'm surprised Adam Merville wasn't on hand to help her, though. You'd think it was easy enough to tear himself away from the Culmore for a short time.'

Ellie had thought about that. Adam seemed a considerate man. Meeting his fiancée at the station and escorting her to Bredon Court would surely have been an obvious thing to do?

She lay down her knife and fork, deep in thought.

Painful Memories

Adam Merville leaned back in his chair, wondering what he was doing here in this smart hotel entertaining a girl who showed little interest in the improvements that had been made to the Culmore Pavilion now nearing completion.

He had been surprised when Marsha phoned from London yesterday to tell him that she was arriving sooner than expected. Of course this was a good thing because it would give them time to get to know one other even though the friends who introduced them at a party on the Thames had filled him in with some of her background.

Her interest in chamber music was good but he couldn't quite imagine petite Marsha going on safari holidays in Africa as they said she had. Even if her shooting was confined to taking photographs it was intriguing to think of her as a huntress.

No doubt Bob and Julie had told Marsha a lot about him, too, that he was recovering from an unhappy relationship that was unfolding even before the accident to his hand meant six months leave from his orchestra. He suspected that Marsha had something to do with his being offered this temporary position at the Culmore.

Bob and Julie had been adamant that he

make the most of Marsha's interest in him since she was the relation of someone still influential in the world of music. Through her he might well have his chance to show his creative talents to people who could help his career.

Since Marsha was a sweet girl and as he was now unattached there was no hardship surely in seeking her company? What did a man like him, with an injured hand that prevented him playing his saxophone, have to lose? Not a lot of course, but there was something too calculating about this for his taste.

However he had been pleased to hear from Marsha and to fall in with her suggestion of sharing a meal together.

Not being familiar with the town, he had left the choice of venue to her and had been dismayed when their taxi drew up at the entrance of The Royal Hotel and he had seen the imposing edifice with its white columns flanking the massive entrance. The girl, Eloise, wouldn't have chosen a place like this. Now why did that thought spring into his mind? He had only met her once or twice but there was something about her that made him feel he had known her always.

The dining-room was situated close to the entrance and there were no steps or awkward doorways for a girl on crutches to contend with. That was as good a reason as any for Marsha to have chosen this place, of course.

As usual his tendency to judge others too quickly had got the better of him.

The attentive waiter had taken in the situation and a table on its own near the wall was at their disposal and Marsha helped into her seat with little fuss.

Adam found he was hungry and settled back to enjoy himself. As they ate he questioned Marsha about her accident, admiring the way she played down the inconvenience. She was here now and that was all that mattered, she told him with a little upward glance from those violet eyes of hers.

He smiled. 'I'm glad to have an opportunity like this for us to meet each other away from the Culmore, Marsha.'

Her responding smile was delightful and a small dimple appeared in her right cheek every now and again as she tilted her face. He could have wished, though, that she was more receptive to what he had to tell her about the improvements at the pavilion, but that, no doubt, would come later.

Her journey today under difficult circumstances must have been exhausting. After a good night's rest her enthusiasm for the project ahead of them would hopefully be in full force. He looked forward to that.

Marsha ran her eye down the list of desserts on the menu, reading them out loud. He found this slightly irritating but then rebuked himself

'The cheeseboard for me, please,' he said

'And you, Marsha?'

He assumed her choice would be for something frothy and was surprised when she opted for the bread and butter pudding with custard. Once again his first impression of her had let him down. He was losing his touch.

'My favourite,' she said, her voice firm.

He looked at her thoughtfully. Decisive. No doubt about that and a good thing in someone in charge of a prestigious art exhibition. He needed someone positive, capable of making instant decisions. All the same a little voice in the back of his mind suggested that some give and take was necessary, because both festivals, music and art, had of necessity to be run in conjunction with each another.

Somehow he had the strong impression that Marsha wasn't going to take kindly to the idea.

*   *   *

Ellie pressed the bell to her old apartment, waited for a few moments and then tried again. So the bell wasn't working or had been disconnected. This would need seeing to. She tapped loudly on the door instead.

Her employer had assured her that Marsha was up and about this morning because she had telephoned earlier and discovered that this was so. She had told her niece that Ellie would soon be on her way down for their preliminary meeting and she hoped Marsha would find everything in order.

Ellie hoped so, too. She moved her heavy file from one arm to the other and tried again. She was rewarded this time by a faint 'Come in for goodness' sake. The door's unlocked.'

She obeyed with care, unsure of her reception. She knew that Marsha had come back late the evening before because she had caught a glimpse of Adam Merville's tall figure as he paid off the taxi outside Bredon Court. Seeing him had given her a strange twist of the heart and she had waited in the shadows until he had accompanied Marsha inside the building and then come out again and gone striding off along the seafront.

Marsha was seated at the table in the living-room, a glass of orange juice in her hand. She looked up as Ellie came in 'You've come to check up on me, have you, to report back to my great-aunt?'

The glint in Marsha's eyes belied the pleasantness of her tone and Ellie felt warmth flood her cheeks. 'I came to see what I could do to help,' she said. 'Your great-aunt thought-you would want to know what's been done about the art exhibition so far.' She looked down at the file she was holding. 'This is for you to glance through, Marsha. If I can be of any further help . . .'

Marsha inclined her head. 'I'm more than able to cope.'

Feeling wrong-footed, Ellie backed towards

the door.

'Wait!' Marsha drained her glass and poured more juice from the jug on the table. 'I need to set a few ground rules before my fiancé and I meet later.'

'Of course.' Ellie looked round for somewhere to deposit the file. 'I have most of the information here, Marsha. Is there somewhere you'd like me to put it?'

Marsha shrugged. 'Dump it in the office if you must. You'll have done the groundwork and sorted out the people who want to exhibit their work, made lists, that sort of thing? My fiancé doesn't expect me to be bothered with the trivialities.'

'Trivialities?'

'The day-to-day boring things.'

'I see.' Ellie thought of the letters to be sent individually to all the artists with instructions for the stewarding of the exhibitions, the arranging for the hiring of screens on which to hang the paintings and assembling a hanging committee of people who knew what they were about. She had expected Marsha to be interested in doing all this, but it sounded very much as if she had no intention of being any more than a figurehead. So why had she been so eager to organise the exhibition in the first place?

'You understand what I'm talking about?'

'I think so. Miss Valence has asked me to help you all I can and of course I will. But my

43

main duties are seeing to her welfare and that must come first.'

Marsha stirred a little in her seat. 'My great-aunt seems to think she's the power behind the Culmore set-up. It could be irksome if she expects to have a say in it all. My fiancé agrees with me.'

'Adam?'

Marsha's eyes narrowed. '*Adam*?'

Ellie flushed. 'Mr Merville.'

Marsha waved her hand. 'We certainly don't want any interference from her. My fiancé is quite adamant about that.'

'He is? He seemed to respect her a great deal the other day and to understand how much it all means to her.'

'I think I know my fiancé's wishes better than anyone'

'But I can't believe he would dismiss your great-aunt's interests just like that.'

'I think you better had,' Marsha spat out.

Ellie bit back a sharp retort. This needed thinking about. Miss Valence was providing her niece with suitable accommodation and also offering the assistance of her employee. She was making things as easy for Marsha as she could. She had no idea of the ingratitude now being poured forth and it would upset her a great deal if she knew.

Marsha leaned forward to reach for the packet of cereal. She looked at it critically and then put it down again. 'So is that all? I'm

44

needed over the road shortly. And, before you stick your nose in. I'm perfectly capable of getting across there under my own steam and you can tell my meddling great-aunt exactly that.'

Ellie made good her escape and leaned against the wall outside, taking several deep breaths to calm her feelings of outrage. Even to please his fiancée would a man like Adam Merville condone Marsha's acid comments about Miss Valence let alone agree with them? She had a brief vision of his expression when he talked of her employer's deep interest in the coming festival and was sure his sympathy for her wasn't merely pretence.

From inside Mrs Drew's apartment she heard Daisy bark and the familiar sound made Ellie square her shoulders and make for the lift because she had no energy left to use the stairs. The whoosh of it was soothing. Obviously Marsha had no idea exactly what needed to be done to run the art exhibition and had no intention of finding out. She wanted praise and adulation without any effort on her part.

Ellie emerged on to her employer's landing and ran up the narrow staircase to her own apartment. She needed air and fast to clear her head. Opening the window wide, she leaned out and breathed in deeply. Then she picked up a used mug left on the window-sill, looked at it with dislike and put it down hard.

45

The satisfying thump was wonderful.

*　　　*　　　*

'So all is well?' Miss Valence said when Ellie joined her. 'I expect Marsha plans to rest today after all the excitement yesterday.'

Ellie smiled and made a non-committal remark. 'She and her fiancé are meeting at the Culmore this morning,' she added.

'Do you think they'd like me to be there, too?'

There was a hint of hope in her employer's voice that pained Ellie as she started to clear the breakfast table. She turned her back for a moment so that Miss Valence wouldn't see her expression. 'I think this first professional meeting is just to gather a few thoughts,' she said when she was more composed. 'Marsha seems to like being independent. She insists on getting herself across there on her own.'

'Oh dear, is that wise? Of course she'll have Adam to escort her back afterwards. A pleasant young man, so kind and considerate.'

Ellie nodded and thought of the first time she had met him and his amusement at discovering her dancing on the back lawn and his wish to help with the guinea pigs when she was finding it difficult to get into her sandals and hold her pets at the same time. Even to please his fiancée would a man like Adam be insensitive to the needs of an old lady like Miss

46

Valence and accuse her of being an interfering busybody? She didn't think so.

She would call for Daisy presently and together they would roam the beach, the dog skittering along the water's edge chasing gulls while she followed slowly trying to decide what she was going to do about Marsha and her unsuspecting great-aunt.

'I should like to have my grandfather's scrapbook to hand,' Miss Valence said 'Would you mind getting it for me, Ellie? It's such a precious thing and I expect Marsha would be so glad to look at it with me when she's rested. It should be in the bureau over there.'

'Of course.' Ellie knew exactly where the scrapbook was and how much her employer valued the record her proud grandfather had kept of her career as a concert pianist from newspaper cuttings and family photographs. She knew, too, the pride Miss Valence felt that she was connected through her grandfather with the opening of the Culmore Pavilion so long ago. Naturally she would expect her niece to feel the same family pride in the building.

Ellie lifted the heavy album and placed it on the table at her employer's side.

'Thank you, Ellie, dear. I shall enjoy this.' She opened a page at random and gave an explanation of pleasure. 'I'd forgotten that this was in here.'

She sounded so pleased that Ellie bent over her shoulder to look. She saw a figure of a man

47

in black and white, tall and broad-shouldered and wearing a suit not unlike the one Adam was wearing when she first saw him. The man was Adam! But how could this be? The likeness was uncanny.

'Who is that?' she asked in wonder.

'Someone very special,' Miss Valence said, a catch in her voice. 'A violist, a brilliant player.'

'He looks so much like Adam.'

'You noticed that?'

Ellie nodded. How could she miss it? There was the same way of standing with his shoulders held straight, the curve to the mouth.

'His name was Edgar. Edgar Whitlock. I cared for him a great deal. He died, you see, in the Second World War, shot down over Italy. A great loss, a very great loss.'

Ellie was unable to speak for a moment for the rush of tears to her throat. She wondered that her employer wasn't similarly affected but merely looked down at the photograph with a sad smile on her lips.

'I'm so pleased you can see Adam's resemblance to him. I see a lot of myself in Marsha too . . . Marsha and Adam a dream come true.'

Miss Valence turned the page and the confidence was over. Saddened, Ellie left her with her memories. She was pleased that Miss Valence had a happy hour or two ahead of her and that she was spared for the moment from

48

knowing her great-niece's true feelings and in how little esteem Marsha held her.

* * *

So, what was she to do for the best? Ellie threw the ball she had brought for Daisy and paused to watch the skill with which the dog retrieved it.

Being a dog was easy, she thought, knowing what had to be done and then doing it. She dreaded witnessing her employer's hurt on discovering Marsha's opinion of her and yet was it kind to keep her in ignorance?

Ellie threw the ball again but this time Daisy, intent on some mission of her own, wasn't interested. Walking across to discover what the dog had found, Ellie saw it was a cuttlefish the tide had brought in. Daisy picked it up in her mouth and looked up at her.

'A present for your mistress?' Ellie said, smiling.

Daisy wagged her tail and they set off up the beach to climb the steps to the promenade. Ellie attached the lead, Daisy waiting patiently with her trophy gripped in her mouth.

No haze lingered round Beachy Head today, an unchanging feature on this part of the coast whether she could see it or not. She wished she could be certain about what she should do. How would she feel if she was in her employer's position, loving and trusting her ungrateful niece?

At the entrance to Bredon Court Ellie stopped in surprise as she saw Adam Merville about to ring the bell. A frisson of happiness shot through her at seeing him when she least expected it.

'Well met,' he said. He stooped to stroke Daisy.

The dog laid her offering at his feet and looked up into his face, tail wagging.

He picked it up. 'Is this for me?'

'This is bizarre,' Ellie said in wonder. 'You're definitely honoured. Poor Mrs Drew will feel sidelined.'

'Not if she knows nothing about it,' he said, smiling, as he slipped the cuttlefish into his jacket pocket.

'You've scored a hit there,' Ellie acknowledged as she opened the door and indicated he should come inside. 'But where's Marsha? Have you just brought her back?'

He looked bewildered. 'Should I have?'

'After your meeting at the Culmore?'

There was silence. Ellie cleared her throat and was startled at how loud the sound was in the quiet entrance hall. But asking a simple question shouldn't make her feel this awkward. Had she put her foot in it again?

'I don't quite understand,' he said.

'The meeting this morning at the Culmore that Marsha was talking about?'

He smiled. Not guilty, I assure you. And we

didn't meet anywhere else today, either,' he said 'Although it might have been pleasant to do so.'

She stared at him.

'I'm here on the off-chance of seeing Miss Valence. Can that be arranged at short notice?'

'I'm sure it can,' Ellie said 'But I'll need to check with her first. Could you wait here while I go up and see? I can't phone her from down here because I'm on the top floor now and I haven't got my mobile with me.'

He raised his eyebrows. 'The top floor . . . you mean the attics?'

'More or less.'

'With no phone connection to Miss Valence's apartment in case of emergency?'

'Well, no.'

She registered his expression of concern as she moved to enter the lift, Daisy obediently at her side. As the doors closed there was a low whine near her feet. Daisy! What could she have been thinking of to forget her.

A short while later they were down again. Adam was examining a print of the Culmore on the wall near the cubbyholes for the mail and turned as the lift doors opened.

'Miss Valence is looking forward to seeing you if you'd like to go up,' Ellie said 'I won't be long taking Daisy back to her owner.'

He nodded. 'I need to see Miss Valence alone today, but I won't take up much of her time.'

'Alone?' she said faintly and then turned away to hide the mounting colour in her face. What business was it of hers? She wasn't her employer's keeper.

A Lie Exposed

Out in the back garden Ginette was slashing at the long grass in the flower-bed nearest to the apartments as if it had done her a terrible wrong. Ellie, on the way to feed her pets, stopped and stared in astonishment.

Ginette swung round.

'Guess who ordered me to do this!'

Ellie smothered a smile.

'I know you always mow the lawn but it's my garden, or as good as. I order you to stop ill-treating it immediately.'

Ginette's responding laugh turned into a hiccup. 'Try telling madam that.'

'Not Marsha?'

'The same.'

Ellie transferred her bag of guinea pig food from one arm to the other. 'But I don't understand,' she said 'Why should it matter to her?'

'She says it looks untidy.'

'And?'

'Apparently it doesn't suit.'

Ellie bit it back a facetious remark as she saw how genuinely upset Ginette was. 'Here, give me that thing,' she said. She took the scythe from her and dumped it and the pet food near the rose trellis. 'I'll see to it myself in my own good time. Meanwhile, coffee good and hot. And what's more, we'll carry it out here to drink it.'

The small kitchenette at the end of the hall was proving useful to Ellie since she had moved out of her apartment, because it saved a journey up to her rooms on the top floor each time she needed to wash her hands. She kept an electric kettle here, too, as well as mugs and a jar of coffee. The small worktop fridge was handy for storing milk and luckily there was some there today.

'So,' Ellie said as they waited for the kettle to boil. 'When did our friend Marsha nobble you for scything duty?'

Ginette shrugged. 'Miss Valence asked me to go down and see what cleaning she needed doing and that was it.'

'Funny sort of cleaning?.

'Blackmail, not cleaning,' Ginette said gloomily. 'Wonder Girl threatened to tell Miss Valence I'd been rude to her if I didn't get that grass cut at once. I didn't like the tone of her voice.'

'And definitely not what she said.'

'No way. I was a fool not to call her bluff.'

Ellie frowned as she made the coffee.

'Grab hold of yours,' she said as she added milk to the two mugs. 'This needs thinking about.'

So Marsha was causing trouble already, she thought as they went out into the garden. She could just picture the scene . . . Miss Valence staring at her niece in disbelief as she accused Ginette of answering back. She would try to reason with Marsha, trembling a little in her anxiety to be fair to them both. And afterwards one of her bad migraine headaches would start and she would be laid low for the rest of the day.

The scythe was on the grass by the trellis where Ellie had left it. She picked it up and swung it back and forth experimentally.

'You look as if you'd like to attack someone with that,' Ginette said.

'Wouldn't I just?'

'That's my girl.'

Ellie laughed. 'I feel better just thinking it.'

'Good for you.'

Ginette sat down on the low wall edging the patio and held both hands round her coffee mug.

Ellie put hers down on a paving stone out of the way of Ginette's swinging foot and set to work on the offending grass. When the job was done she stood for a moment breathing deeply. 'That will have to do for the moment,' she said 'I'll weed the bed properly by hand later on Please, Ginette, don't get into any

54

fights with Marsha. I'll have a word with her myself.'

'And tell her what . . . that she's to stop bullying her great-aunt's poor little delicate cleaning lady or she's for the high jump? I can't see our Wonder Girl taking that on board.'

Ellie smiled as she sat down on the wall. 'I shan't be quite as blunt as that. Subtle, that's me.'

'And the best of luck,' Ginette said, her usual good temper restored.

Out here in the sunshine it was easy for Ellie to think she could convince Marsha that, since the garden was her responsibility, she was the one in charge and would work on it in her own good time. It was fortunate that Ginette, usually so quick to argue, hadn't rounded on Marsha on this occasion.

'You think I need luck?' she said.'And how.'

Ellie smiled and then gazed thoughtfully at the ground floor windows as she drank her coffee. Marsha seemed determined to make her presence felt, but what possible need was there for that? She was Miss Valence's great-niece, her only relative as she had been quick to point out, ensconced in the ground floor flat here at Bredon Court and the organiser of the art exhibition. A person with authority anyone would say. And not only that but she would get the opportunity of meeting with Adam Merville on a daily basis.

Now where had that thought come from? Startled, Ellie tried to banish Adam from her mind but somehow a vision of him smiling at her as he pocketed Daisy's gift of a cuttlefish stayed with her.

* * *

'Adam phoned soon after he left here,' Miss Valence said.

'He did?' Ellie looked at her employer enquiringly. 'He needed to ask you something?'

'He wants to see you later this morning, Ellie, in the committee room at the Culmore at twelve-thirty. He knew he couldn't phone you direct so he asked me to give the message to you.'

'I'll be there,' Ellie promised. She picked up Miss Valence's empty coffee cup and turned to go, surprised at the warmth that filled her knowing she would see him again so soon.

'One minute, Ellie,' Miss Valence said 'I spoke to Marsha earlier and she seemed a little down. I wonder if you'd call on her and see if she needs anything? Her fiancé was asking after her, wondering if she were quite well. He ..' She broke off, faint colour tingeing her lined cheeks and her eyes not quite meeting Ellie's gaze. 'At least I'm quite sure he would have if he had thought of it Such a considerate young man . . . so much like . . .'

56

Again she broke off and Ellie hardly knew what to say. She cleared her throat and the sound in the quiet room seemed to cure Miss Valence of whatever it was that was troubling her

'Of course I'll call on her,' she said 'I'll need to get the file from the office anyway and carry it over for her as it's so heavy.'

Ellie had tried to sound confident about this, but as she tapped on the door of the apartment downstairs she wondered what reception she would get. There was no way, on crutches, that Marsha would be able to manage the file herself'

Ellie tried the handle and found the door locked. She should have thought about something like this and got another key organised for when she needed to use the office. She would see to it as soon as she got back from the Culmore.

*   *   *

Adam drummed the fingers of his right hand on the desk in front of him, reminded suddenly of his growing suspicion that Miss Valence regarded him as a prospective suitor for her great-niece's hand. She had asked him particularly to keep his eye on Marsha but he had made it clear at once that since he had become involved with the festival at such a late stage his time would be limited.

He let out a shout of laughter. Miss Valence's obvious intention was going too far even for his dear friends' sake. Bob and Julie hardly knew Marsha after all. In any case he intended to plan his future for himself and no amount of coercion on Miss Valence's part would have the slightest effect on him.

He looked up and smiled as Ellie knocked lightly on the open door of the committee room and went inside. She had expected to see Marsha seated there, too, and her absence was a surprise.

'Come in, Eloise. Thank you for coming.' He half stood up and indicated the chair opposite him at the table. 'I need to get a few things clear from you before I meet with the festival committee this afternoon so I'm not at a disadvantage. Marsha won't have got her head round it all yet.'

His short-sleeved shirt was open at the neck and his skin seemed to shine with energy, and warmth. He looked as if he had been here for hours working hard.

Ellie sat down and gazed down at her hands as if examining them for the information he needed and, looking up again, caught a gleam of amusement in his eyes. Discomforted, she moved slightly 'I'm sorry I haven't got the information file with me,' she said.

'That would have been useful.'

She cleared her throat. 'I'll make sure I have it next time.'

58

'So you're not so efficient after all?'

She felt herself flush at the hint of laughter in his voice and frowned, unable to respond to his obvious teasing because she felt the fault was hers. 'The file is kept in the office over the road and that's one of the rooms in the ground floor apartment.'

He raised his eyebrows. 'And?'

'I can't get them at the moment because Marsha appears to be out. I thought she might be here.'

He shrugged. 'Not to worry. Next time will do. Just fill me in about what's been done so far.'

Ellie did so, leaning back in her chair. The file was Marsha's responsibility now so why was she feeling guilty when there was no need?

Adam nodded approval once or twice as he made notes of what Ellie said. She hadn't noticed before that he held his biro in his left hand rather awkwardly. She watched as it moved slowly across the paper.

Then he looked up and smiled. 'Everything seems to be going well.'

'But a bit behind schedule,' she admitted. 'That will alter now Marsha's here, of course. The next step is getting all the helpers together to meet her and for her to allocate the responsibilities.'

'You've organised this sort of thing before?'

She shook her head. 'I'm learning as I go and just starting things off so that your fiancée

59

can take over.'

'My fiancée?'

She looked at him in surprise.

'What did you mean when you said that, Ellie?' he said. 'Surely you can't think I have a secret fiancée stashed away here?'

'Marsha?' she said, her mouth dry.

He looked bewildered. 'There's obviously a mistake. Marsha and I have no such understanding. In fact we've only met a couple of times. Hardly time to get acquainted let alone to be making long-term plans for spending the rest of our lives together.' He was serious suddenly. 'At least I hope not.'

For a moment he looked haunted. She longed to reassure him that a man like him would have no difficulty fighting his own battles. But how could she know this? She bit her lip, considering.

There was moment's silence. Ellie felt her cheeks glow and knew she was incapable of speech for the next few seconds because of the way Adam was gazing at her

'So who told you this?' he said at last.

She hesitated, not wanting to reply in case she came out with something else as stupid as this appeared to be. The assumption wasn't her fault, but she wished she hadn't made it.

'Marsha seemed to give that impression,' she said.

'And you jumped to the wrong conclusion?'

'It wasn't like that,' she said, feeling

uncomfortable. 'Marsha referred to you as her fiancé to Miss Valence as well as to me. Why should we doubt it?'

'Why, indeed?' His eyes narrowed. 'It seems that Marsha and I need to have a little talk.'

They discussed other arrangements for the exhibition after that and as soon as their meeting finished Ellie was out of her chair, ready to make her escape. She paused at the door and looked back, surprising an enigmatic expression on Adam's face. Was he flattered that Marsha wanted them to assume that she and Adam meant a great deal to each other? Many men would be. From his point of view her foolish words might be a blessing in disguise.

The thought was so painful that she dashed across the road without looking and narrowly missed colliding with a boy on a mountain bike pretending he was a racing driver. Her ears ringing with his shouts of outrage and with burning cheeks, she let herself into Bredon Court.

*   *   *

'It's not a hanging offence,' Ginette said cheerfully. She reached inside the cupboard on the top landing where she stored her sailing gear and pulled out her life jacket.

'It felt like it,' Ellie said. 'So what did Miss

61

Valence say about the phantom engagement?'

'I haven't told her yet. I need to think about it first before I say anything. Marsha made it clear to both of us that she and Adam were engaged. At least, I think she did. I'm not sure of anything anymore.'

'Weird,' Ginette said.

'But why?'

'Because she's mad. Mad, bad and horrible to know.'

Ellie shrugged. 'You could be right there. But it's her problem and Adam's now. They'll have to sort it out.'

Ginette giggled. 'I wish I could be a fly on the wall when they do. I wonder what she'll say to him?'

She sounded so gleeful that Ellie laughed, feeling the tension seep out of her.

Ellie smiled. 'I meant to ask you . . . how's that fellow of yours?'

Ginette tried to look puzzled and failed. 'Come over to the sailing club and meet Sam this evening why don't you, Ellie? We're having a bit of a get-together . . drinks and nibbles to celebrate our hundredth new member. David somebody. I'm sure I've seen him somewhere before.'

'A hundred members? That many?'

'Don't look so surprised. You could have been one of them if you hadn't chickened out.'

Ellie laughed.

'That's the spirit, girl. And now I must rush.

Sam's getting my boat rigged and ready for me, the lovely lad.'

*　　　*　　　*

Marsha returned to Bredon Court in mid afternoon. Ellie heard a car draw up outside as she finished weeding the condemned flower-bed on her hands and knees. From the sound of Marsha's voice she assumed she had used a taxi. Had it been anyone else she would have gone out to offer assistance but knew better than to do that now.

She sat back on her heels and listened as a car engine started up. A few moments later the sash window of her old apartment crashed open and Marsha's head appeared.

'What are you doing?' she demanded.

Stung by the peremptory tone Ellie didn't answer for moment. She pulled out the last root of dandelion and put it in the pile for her guinea pigs. The she looked up. 'I'm weeding my flower-bed,' she said.

'Since when?'

'About two o'clock.'

'I want to see you. *Now.*'

The window slammed down. No prizes for guessing that Marsha had met Adam and the resulting interview had not been good for her. Relieved about that, Ellie thought briefly of Ginette out there on the waves with not a care in the world and wished she was out there, too. She didn't take kindly to Marsha's bossy summons, although she saw no way of voiding it.

She got to her feet to return her gardening tools to the shed near the back door. In the circumstances she should have known better than to give a facetious answer to Marsha's interrogation but she hadn't been able to resist it.

She ran the hot tap longer than was necessary and then had to add enough cold water be able to plunge her hands in without scalding them.

Until Marsha's angry words just now she hadn't allowed herself to believe that Adam's denial of an engagement wasn't just wishful thinking on her part. Now her veins coursed with warmth that he wasn't in thrall, after all, to a selfish girl likely to make his life a misery. The coming interview was surely a small price to pay for knowing that.

She took a deep breath and went out into the hall. Marsha was waiting there, leaning against the mail cubby holes for support with her crutches at her side and glaring at her so ferociously that Ellie took a step back.

'I've just been to see Adam Merville,' Marsha said accusingly. 'What's this ridiculous thing you've been telling him? So when did *I* tell you he and I were engaged to be married?'

'Ridiculous?'

'Yes, ridiculous.'

64

Ellie looked at her steadily, trying to fathom Marsha's game. It was a crazy thing to have done because she was sure to be found out sooner or later. Obviously the time had come sooner than expected.

'You can't answer that, can you?' Marsha said with triumph. 'Because it didn't happen.'

'No? I understood that was the reason you wanted to be in Cheselton, so you could work with Adam on the music and art festival,' Ellie said as calmly as she could manage.

Marsha picked up one of her crutches. 'And who gave you that idea? No, don't tell me. I'm fully aware of my great-aunt's embarrassing blunder. You can't take an old woman's maunderings for gospel truth. You should know that, having worked for her for months.'

'I know nothing of the sort,' Ellie said with spirit.

'Then you're more stupid that I gave you credit for.'

'There's nothing wrong with Miss Valence's intellect. In fact, it's a lot sharper than most people's of her age.'

'Oh? So what made her come out with such a preposterous lie?'

'A lie? I heard you refer to Adam as your fiancé with my own ears.'

'So who would believe you? I put things right on that score with Adam at once, I can tell you. We had a good laugh about

65

it together. You should curb your feverish imagination or it'll get you in trouble one day if it hasn't already. It's clear to everyone what your little game is.'

'*My* game? That's preposterous.'

'Preposterous, is it? So why is your face so red?'

Ellie was speechless at the venom in Marsha's voice. She put up her hands to rub her cheeks.

Marsha gave a scornful laugh. 'I suppose I should be flattered that my great-aunt is trying to warn you off making a play for Adam Merville by pretending he's already spoken for Maybe she's not such a fool as she looks. And you needn't think working for her gives you any advantages as far as he's concerned.'

'I'm not listening to any more of this,' Ellie said/ She ran up the stairs to her rooms at the top of the house at such speed that she had to pause outside her door to regain her breath.

*　　　*　　　*

Seated at her table, Ellie rested her chin in her hands. Uppermost in her mind now was deep concern for Miss Valence. It would hurt her deeply to know that Marsha was capable of any manner of lies and deceit and she didn't know how she was going to protect her from that. She would have to warn her that Marsha and Adam no longer planned to marry of course, but maybe her employer need never know of the part she had unknowingly played in the mix-up of the fake engagement. Unless Marsha attacked her great-aunt verbally about it, of course. But bow likely was that when she knew she was in the wrong?

Somehow she must make sure it didn't happen.

Marsha's disinterest in the Culmore Pavilion and her wish to have little to do in the organisation of the art exhibition was a different matter. Would it be better for her employer to come to terms with that now or could that be hidden from her for as long as possible? But what then? Miss Valence might well feel cheated and humiliated if she stumbled on the truth in the future and knew that Ellie had known this all along and failed to tell her about it.

Ellie sighed, uncertain of how she should handle it.

Visitors

The bell to the ground floor apartment rang as Ellie finished printing out some letters in the office next day.

'Get that will you?' Marsha called from her sitting room. 'Or ignore it. It won't be anyone important.'

'I can't do that.' Ellie said, getting up from her chair.

'Anxious to keep well in with my great-aunt?'

Ellie ignored her. Outside the apartment looking slightly out of place in their smart clothes, were her father and Amanda.

'Dad!' she cried, almost falling into his arms. She turned to Amanda and gave her a hug, too. 'What a lovely surprise!'

'You haven't been checking your answer phone, love,' her father said. 'We left a message to say we'd be calling in on our way home from the airport.'

'You did?' Ellie felt her colour rise with annoyance that Marsha hadn't told her.

'Can we come in?' Amanda said.

She was looking very pretty in a jacket that was the same shade of pink as the roses she held out to Ellie.

Seeing Ellie hesitate, her father looked anxious. 'Is everything all right, love?' he asked, his voice deep with concern.

'Who is it?' Marsha called in a sharp tone. 'Tell them to come in, or go away.'

Amanda took a step back. 'Haven't we come to the right place?'

'Of course you have,' Ellie said quickly. 'It's just that this isn't my apartment any more. I'm upstairs now.'

She heard the sound of Marsha's crutches knock against the door jamb as she came to see what was going on.

'This is Miss Valence's great-niece, Marsha,' Ellie said. 'Marsha, my parents John and Amanda Langley.'

'Are you really Miss Valence's great-niece?' Amanda said. She opened her eyes wide in surprise. 'The old lady must be very old.'

Ellie smiled at Amanda's artless words. She hoped that Marsha wouldn't take them amiss.

But Marsha looked delighted. 'She's very elderly,' she said with satisfaction. 'And so frail. I do all I can for her, of course.'

'And you only a slip of a thing yourself,' John Langley said warmly 'But we mustn't keep you standing there on those crutches, my dear. An accident, was it? Ellie hasn't told us about that.'

A brave smile touched Marsha's lips. 'It's not important to anyone else, you see. And I'm managing so well on my own.'

John Langley looked approving. 'Well done my dear.'

Amanda tilted her fair head back and was gazing about her, obviously awed by the splendour of the high ceiling and the decorative plasterwork. 'It's such a lovely building,' she said 'What a beautiful place to live.'

'I think so,' Marsha said.

Ellie felt a surge of irritation at her smug expression as if she had it all planned to her advantage. Maybe she had even decided that her great-aunt's luxury apartment would suit her needs better?

'I wish I could live here for the rest of my life,' she said. Again the vulnerable smile.

Ellie bit her lip as she saw how readily her father was falling for Marsha's charm. It was a relief when she managed to get him and Amanda into the lift and up to her loft apartment.

Dad smiled kindly at Ellie as he removed his jacket and sat down at the table. 'Everything going well, love?' he said 'You're looking a bit down.'

Ellie nodded as she made tea the way they liked it, with a slice of lemon for Amanda and a lot of milk and two teaspoons of sugar for Dad. 'I'm fine,' she said.

Amanda was still holding the flowers and she looked down at them now. 'We know how much you like roses, Ellie,' she said 'Pink and white and pale lemon . . . not like these really. But . . .'

'Stop babbling, Amanda my love,' John Langley said fondly

'Let me put them in water,' Ellie said. She took them from her and buried her face in their delicate scent for a moment, anxious of what Dad and Amanda might be going to tell her.

'We just felt like seeing you, Ellie,' her father said after a silence that went on a little too long for comfort. 'Never having seen the place,' he added. 'Or met your Miss Valence.'

'That can be arranged quite easily,' Ellie said 'But first tell me all that's been happening. How was Provence?'

Amanda's eyes looked dreamy as she told her of hot days by the pool, the mountains in the distance and the sweet smell of thyme. When she finished and they had asked Ellie about the music festival and the art exhibition she ran down to her employer's apartment to ask if she would like to meet them.

'Of course, my dear,' Miss Valence said 'And then afterwards you must take time off to show them round the Culmore and then give them lunch somewhere nice. Mrs Drew has just phoned to say she's coming up to see me and bringing a quiche she's made so there's no need to worry about me. You deserve a little holiday, my dear, and if you go to the Avalon and mention my name the manager will charge the meal to my account.'

Overcome by her generosity, Ellie leaned

forward and kissed her cheek. 'They'll love you as much as I do,' she said.

*　　*　　*

After a lengthy tour of the Culmore Pavilion they were glad to relax in the comfortable surroundings of the small hotel along the sea front. Amanda went at once to the powder room and Ellie's father, looking suddenly worn, leaned back in his chair and sighed.

'You're all right, aren't you Dad?' Ellie asked.

'Me? As right as rain,' he said 'You're the one we need to be anxious about. I have a feeling there's something going on that's worrying you, Ellie. It wouldn't have anything to do with that selfish madam in your apartment, would it?'

Ellie felt a sudden lump in her throat at his understanding. 'Marsha?'

'That's the one.'

'The one what?' Amanda said, slipping back into her seat.

'The imposter posing as the old lady's great-niece.'

Ellie laughed. 'She's no imposter.'

'Not in that sense, perhaps,' he said 'But she's ousted my lovely daughter from her flat.'

'Only because she has a broken ankle and it's more convenient for her now she's come to run the art festival side of things.'

Her father raised his eyebrows. 'So there's no lift in the building? I could have sworn we travelled up here in one.'

Amanda pulled her pretty skirt down over her knees. 'She has such gorgeous blonde hair and she's so slim it's not fair,' she said

'But you're slim, too, my love. At the moment.'

'But she's on crutches, too. Enough to melt the heart.'

'I hope you don't mean me?' John said.

She smiled at him. 'No?'

'She's got her eye on the main chance, that one,' he said. 'Did you see the confident way she gazed round the entrance hall as if she owned the place already, as she is obviously planning to do in due course?'

Amanda sighed. 'Her great-aunt's a sweetie.'

'I'm glad you like Miss Valence,' Ellie said, warmed by Dad's agreement with own suspicions about Marsha.

'Of course I like her,' Amanda said. 'And Marsha will make a lovely friend for you Ellie.'

John Langley glanced at his young wife. 'You think so?'

Ellie let it go. 'Miss Valence has been kind to me,' she said as the waiter approached their table with the menu.

'So why the sad look?' her father asked after they had each made their choice.

Instantly Ellie sat up straight and smiled at him. 'You're imagining things, Dad.'

The meal was excellent, and afterwards they walked along the seafront and sat on a seat to watch a couple of sailing dinghies out on the water, their sails tilted a little in the breeze.

'I'm so glad we came to see you Ellie,' Amanda said. Ellie smiled at her. 'Me, too.'

Her father glanced at his watch. 'We'll need to get going soon, Ellie, my love, but we'll certainly come again when we can. We may not be able to make the Culmore opening but we'll do our best, won't we, Amanda, love?'

Amanda nodded.

Ellie had the feeling that there was something they weren't telling her about. She looked enquiringly at her father.

'Nothing for you to worry about, Ellie,' he said. 'It's just the way it is. And make sure you watch out for that girl. She's out to do you no good.'

Ellie walked back to the car park with them and waved them off with a sad heart. Then she walked thoughtfully back to Bredon Court. She felt comforted that Dad sympathised with her growing suspicion that her employer's niece might be planning something that would hurt her deeply. And that something, she suspected, involved Adam.

She wished she could have introduced him to Dad but apparently Adam had been called away for a few hours. If it wasn't crazy to think so she might have imagined that Marsha was behind that.

74

To come face to face with him when she was in sight of the Culmore was something Ellie hadn't expected. He was glancing at his watch and looked so astonished to see her that she smiled.

'So you haven't gone off with your relations for a few nights in the big city after all,' he said

'Should I have done?'

'Well, no, not if you changed your mind.'

It was never on the agenda,' she said 'My work is here with Miss Valence. I had no plans to abscond.'

'Marsha must have got it wrong then.'

Like a few other things, she felt like saying. He looked just as he always did with not a mark on him. She half-expected a scratched face, bruises beneath his eyes, evidence of Marsha's spiteful retaliation when he denied their engagement and not seeing them smiled at herself.

She was telling me that you insist on serving nibbles at the art preview?

She looked at him in surprise. 'I do? But would that be a problem?'

'She considers it unstylish, I understand?'

Ellie's lips twitched. 'I wasn't going to suggest pink tinned salmon on cream crackers. Or hunks of stale bread filled with mouldy cheese.'

He laughed. 'Hardly. But she feels strongly that wine only should be served and that anything else would be a waste of money.'

'No tapas then, no smoked salmon on tiny blinis, no stuffed olives or delicious dips or delicate crab open sandwiches?'

'You're making me feel hungry.'

'Me, too,' she said, her eyes dancing. 'And now I must see to my employer's evening meal. *You* join in Miss Valence and me if you like . . .' She broke off, aghast. What had made her come out with that?'

'Better still, why don't I take you both out somewhere? I've discovered a charming place I think she would like. Would that be possible?'

She felt warmth flood through her and hoped it didn't show in her face. 'I think she'd like that. I'll ask her at once and let you know'

'Do that I'll look forward to it.'

'Me, too,' she said.

And that was the understatement of the year, she thought as they parted. She would shower and wash her hair as soon as they contacted Adam to accept his invitation and then spend the rest of the time assisting Miss Valence with her finery so she looked her best for a delightful evening out.

Ellie walked the rest of the way as if floating a couple of inches above the ground, wondering where Adam would take them.

Miss Valence rarely left her home without

76

assistance and Ellie could hardly believe she wasn't here now. Her first thought was an accident, an ambulance summoned, alarm bells ringing as it rushed her off to hospital. Then she took a deep breath and did the sensible thing and picked up the phone to dial Marsha's number.

The ringing tone stopped and the answer phone cut in. Startled, Ellie left a message and then went to the window and looked down at the garden in the hope that Miss Valence and her niece were out there in the sunshine. They weren't, so where were they?

She jumped as the phone rang.

'Ellie Langley?'

She took a deep breath. 'Marsha?'

'Since you saw fit to abandon your duties in that feckless way, I've got my great-aunt down here with me.'

'Miss Valence is there? May I speak to her?'

'I'll take a message.'

'I need a reply about something.'

'And?'

Ellie hesitated, knowing she had no option but to relay Adam's invitation to Miss Valence and herself through Marsha. She concentrated on steadying her voice, afraid of the listener's reaction.

After a short silence Marsha's voice was sharper than before. 'I suppose this is a ruse to get your hooks into Adam, but it isn't going to work. It's out of the question and always will be?'

'And why is that?'

'My great-aunt is dining here with me this evening and she needs you to be here, too. So the answer's no.'

Ellie replaced the receiver, sick at heart, unable to believe that Miss Valence had. agreed to this so readily.

There was nothing to be done except to dial Adam's number written on the pad alongside the phone and pray that Marsha had the good sense to keep quiet about the ridiculous situation in which she had got herself. Ellie tried to hide the disappointment in her voice as she explained the situation to Adam.

'Please, don't worry about it,' he said, his tone pleasant. 'I'm so sorry.'

'Another time perhaps?'

She replaced the receiver. And that was that. Adam hadn't seemed to mind at all. Why should he? It had been merely an impulse on his part. He might even think she was making excuses not to accept.

She took a deep breath and left the apartment.

A Date Is Cancelled

The take-aways that Marsha sent out for proved to be inedible. In any case Ellie had no appetite. Miss Valence toyed with her chicken korma and then laid down her knife and fork with a sigh.

'Disgusting, isn't it?' Marsha said She sounded uncaring, as if she had other things on her mind.

Ellie hoped they would stay there.

'It's not your fault, my dear.'

Ellie glanced across at her employer and saw that although the meal was disappointing she was enjoying the occasion. Miss Valence was probably more delighted to be here than if they had been dining with Adam because her great-niece, who so far had shown no wish for her company, had taken the trouble to invite her. Her crimson velvet dress gave a glow to her normally pale complexion while Marsha's rather crumpled pale blue top made her look washed-out.

'I've put plenty of ham in the fridge,' Ellie said 'I'll get some, shall I?'

Miss Valence smiled. 'You're a good girl, Ellie.'

As Ellie got up Marsha leaned back in her hair and yawned. She appeared listless this evening as if the effort of having them here was too much for her. Her great-aunt seemed suddenly to notice it, too.

'My dear, you're exhausted.'

'I am, just a little.'

'Then I think we should go. And you'll be glad to bring something for Marsha, I'm sure, Ellie?'

Ellie smiled. Slices of ham doused in the hottest chilli marinade she could invent that would burn the roof of Marsha's mouth? If she dared. 'Of course,' she said, relinquishing this idea with regret. 'I'll be delighted.'

*　　*　　*

Up in her own apartment Miss Valence sat down and leaned back with her eyes closed. The knuckles of her clenched hands on her lap were white. The disappointment at not spending the rest of the evening with her great-niece was only too apparent.

Ellie looked at her anxiously. They never did find out from Marsha what the important thing was she had to tell them. She doubted there ever was one.

'I hope Marsha has thought about the invitations for the preview evening,' Miss Valence murmured when they had eaten the cold repast Ellie prepared. 'Such a lovely social occasion for the public to meet the musicians and artists informally when all the preparation's in place. But I expect she's got it all under control. Has she said anything about them to you, Ellie, my dear?'

Ellie shook her head. She had wondered about making sure of that but Marsha had made it plain that she didn't want any interference. Did this count as interference when it would most likely be her job to contact the printers to arrange for the cards to be printed? 'I'll have a word with her tomorrow,' she promised.

There were other things, too, but she wasn't going to mention them now. Mentally she reviewed the list she had written earlier to remind herself what still needed to be done.

Miss Valence stirred in her chair. 'Do you think Marsha is happy organising the art exhibition, Ellie? I sometimes wonder.'

'I hope so,' Ellie said.

'She had rather a sad childhood, no settled schooling because her father never liked to stay very long in one place. He had been a musician, you know with a career ahead of him with the Cellini Orchestra but he threw it all away.' Her employer's voice was deep with disapproval.

'The Cellini Orchestra?' Ellie said with interest. 'Isn't that the orchestra Adam belonged to?'

'Ah, yes, the Cellini. A link between them, Marsha and Adam. Of course Adam started playing with them many years later. Apparently friends of both brought them together.'

'And Marsha,' Ellie said, anxious to avoid talk of Adam. 'What did she choose to do?'

Miss Valence smoothed the skirt of her dress. 'She was a clever little thing. But something went wrong somewhere. She left school hurriedly and went off to Scotland with her mother and had some sort of breakdown, poor girl. I don't think she ever did any paid work until her mother died and she rejoined her father in London. Since then she's gone from one job to another, never staying long in any of them, just like her father, I'm afraid.' Miss Valence sighed.

Ellie cleared her throat, remembering the love in her own home and the security that gave her. It was hard not to feel sympathy for Marsha.

'I expect you are tired, too, my dear. You're a good girl finding some food for the three of us at short notice. The ham salad was delicious and I expect Marsha thought so, too.'

'I'll collect her dishes in the morning.'

'And I shall retire for the night. I'll see you tomorrow, my dear.'

Ellie left her, but instead of going up to her flat she went down to the dusky garden where the scents of honeysuckle and rambling roses mingled pleasantly and she could breathe in the evening air and wait for its peace to calm her troubled mind.

Perhaps it was as well the meal with Adam hadn't worked out. Inevitably, as it often had since meeting him, she thought of Charles and the trauma of their break-up nearly two years ago. Her love had faded away, killed by his rejection, but the memory of those agonising weeks was still with her. So what was she doing thinking of a man in a way she had vowed never to do again? She had allowed her pleasure in Adam's company, and her wish to get to know him better, to cloud her better judgement. Marsha insisting on her accompanying Miss Valence this evening was a let out for which she should be grateful.

She got up, feeling the sweet grass beneath her feet as she crossed the lawn to the hutch in the corner. She lifted out her pets and held their soft bodies to her face. Now that she knew something of Marsha's history, life was taking on complications for which she hadn't bargained.

*　　*　　*

'He's wonderful,' Ginette said, her eyes dreamy as she dusted the banisters in the entrance hail next morning. Ellie, coming back in from her rainy walk with Daisy, tapped on Mrs Drew's door and handed her over.
'You're wet,' Ginette said.

Ellie took off her jacket and shook the moisture from her hair. 'I'm surprised you noticed, the romantic mood you're in,' she said. 'I suppose you mean Sam?'

'Who else?' Ginette sighed.

'I'm going to put my wet things in the kitchenette before I drip any more on your clean floor. Then stick the kettle on. Ready for coffee?'

'We're going sailing along the coast to Warden Bay this afternoon, Sam and me,' Ginette murmured.

'In this weather?'

Ginette looked surprised. 'Is it raining?'

Ellie gave up getting any sense out of her. She spread her wet jacket over two of the hooks on the wall and then turned her attention to making coffee. Ginette came to join her, sitting on a stool and twining her legs round the upright bars.

The hot drink was welcome and Ellie drank hers as soon as she could, feeling the burning liquid slide down her throat. 'I needed that,' she said.

'I mustn't be long,' Ginette said 'Next on the agenda is cleaning Wonder Girl's pad. Lucky she went out early.'

'Marsha's out in this?'

'Until after lunch, she said. 'That gives us a clear field, the perfect chance to do some serious sleuthing.'

Ellie laughed. 'As if.'

'You're entitled to use the office, aren't you?'

'The office, yes. Marsha's personal space, no.'

Ginette downed her coffee and banged her mug down on the worktop. 'Come on, what are we waiting for?'

She sprang off the stool and made purposely for the door. By the time Ellie caught her up she was at the cupboard in the hall pulling out her cleaning paraphernalia ready for action.

She carried the vacuum cleaner to Marsha's door and tapped loudly. 'Just for appearance's sake,' she said as she turned the door handle and found it unlocked. 'I hope you were joking about not having a look round just now.'

'Hope on, Ginette,' Ellie said, smiling. 'I've got some principles you know and I'm going to stick to them.'

'More fool you.'

Sudden crashing sounds from above made them both look up.

'Sounds like an elephant gone mad,' Ginette said. The noise stopped and then started again.

'I'd better investigate,' Ellie said This was worrying. The two sisters who shared the flat above were normally so quiet she sometimes wondered if they were still in residence.

She ran up the stairs, Ginette following, and arrived breathlessly at their door. She rapped on it and the pounding inside stopped.

'Come in, come in,' someone called impatiently.

'Miss Whitlock sounds all right,' Ginette said. 'Thank goodness for that.'

Relieved, Ellie pushed open the door

85

and saw the younger sister, seventy-year-old Marjorie Lindle, lying flat on her back waving her legs in the air.

Ellie stared in amazement and Ginette let out a shriek of laughter.

'Just exercising, my dears,' Marjorie said as she sat up and smiled at them. 'Did we disturb you?'

'We?' snorted her sister. 'I've got more sense than to take part in this stupid caper at my age.'

'But you should do, dear. It makes me feel ten years younger,' Marjorie said.

'But who wants to look seventy?'

'Sixty in my case, please, Barbara. Look, girls, I can cycle backwards like this.' She lay down again and circled her legs.

'Stuff and nonsense. What would David think of his deranged mother?' Barbara said 'It's enough to put him off coming back here to live.' Barbara Whitlock, her back ramrod-straight, marched out of the room.

'Take no notice of her,' Marjorie said, still working her legs hard. 'If my son can take up dinghy sailing at his age then I can exercise at mine.'

'If you're sure you're all right we'll leave you to it,' Ellie said.

They were giggling as they withdrew and still smiling as they descended to the ground floor. The door to Marsha's apartment stood wide open as they had left it.

86

Ellie's heart leapt to see Adam standing on the threshold. His faded denim shirt and jeans surprised her, too.

He frowned as he saw them. 'What's the meaning of this open door?' he said, his voice suspicious. 'Surely Marsha didn't leave it like this?'

'We thought there was a crisis in the flat upstairs,' Ellie said.

'There were noises,' Ginette added.

'What sort of noises?'

'Of someone exercising,' Ellie said, realising how weak that sounded as soon as the words were out of her mouth.

'And that's a crisis?'

'It might have been.'

'I see.'

That was doubtful, Ellie thought. Surely she didn't have to spell out that the welfare of the Bredon Court residents was her concern?

'Ginette's here to do some cleaning and I need to write some letters for Miss Valence,' she said, wishing she didn't sound so defensive.

Ginette had already carried her vacuum cleaner into the apartment and was busy plugging it in. 'Proof?' she said.

It was no business of his whether or not they had left the door of the apartment wide open or not, Ellie thought. The outside door had been locked as always. No-one could get in unless they had a key. She might have asked what he was doing here, but somehow his assurance as he stood there looking at her so intently made that seem impertinent. 'I'd better get on with my work, too,' she said She tried to open the office door.

'Here, let me.' Adam tried and failed. 'It appears to be locked?'

'Three guesses who did that,' Ginette called from the sitting-room,

Adam ignored her. He cleared his throat, looking awkward. 'I have a lot on my mind,' he said quietly. 'There's something important I need to discuss with you, Ellie. Is there somewhere we can go that's less noisy?'

Ellie thought of her messy and cramped flat on the top floor.

Seeing her hesitation he glanced at his watch. 'They're busy over at the Culmore or we could have gone there, but there would be frequent interruptions. Have you time for a walk further along the sea front?'

She nodded. 'The letters can wait till later. Can you give me ten minutes? I'll have to check with Miss Valence first in case she needs me for anything else.'

'Fine. And thanks, Ellie. I'll wander along to the sailing club and wait for you on one of the seats nearby.'

The noise of the vacuum cleaner stopped abruptly. 'A date is it?' Ginette called as Adam left.

Ellie felt herself flush. 'Get on with your work or you'll have Marsha back before you've finished. I've things to do.'

Ginette's mocking laughter followed her up the stairs.

Concerns Are Raised

Now that the rain had cleared, Ellie, wearing a new pair of jeans and a clean white top, felt her spirits rise as she hurried along the sea front.

She couldn't help a smile spreading across her features when she saw him waiting for her. So what price her resolution to keep hcr distance now? But this was obviously a business meeting, quite in order. She slowed her pace and tried to look suitably serious and business-like.

Adam was staring out to sea though there was nothing out there on the water to warrant his attention.

'Adam!'

He was up in an instant, smiling a welcome.

'I'm sorry I'm a bit late,' she said, breathless for no apparent reason.

'Miss Valence is well?'

'She wanted to know where you were taking me.'

A frown creased his forehead. 'But not why? That's good.'

'Is it all a deep secret?'

'I trust your discretion, Ellie. I'm sure I

89

have that?' She felt a thrill of pleasure at his confidence. 'Of course.'

He nodded. 'Then let's walk'

A silence deepened between them. She wondered why.

'It''s awkward,' he said at last. 'There's a management meeting this afternoon and I have to be there so I don't want to be too far away. But not too near Bredon Court, either.'

'So where are we going?'

'Not far.'

'I see,' she said. He wasn't giving much away and she didn't know why this was important enough for him to whisk her away from Bredon Court.

'They want a full report on the progress so far with the organisation of both the music and the art festivals,' he said. 'The exhibition of paintings, that is.'

'That's reasonable.'

'The arrangements for the music festival are all in place.'

'Ah,' she said, light dawning.

He looked uncertain. 'You understand the difficulty?'

'You mean Marsha still hasn't made up her mind whether or not to have nibbles at the art preview?'

'That's not funny.'

He looked vulnerable suddenly and she was at once contrite. 'Sorry, Adam,' she said.

'Perhaps I deserve that after of accusing you

90

of goodness knows what back at Bredon Court just now?'

'You mean that there's something you want me to help you with?'

'We need to talk this through. Have you time for a sandwich or something, Ellie? I know a place along here where we can be quiet.'

This was a small café not far away, hidden behind a hedge that cut out the light from the small windows facing the road. It was a wonder he had found it, hidden away as it was.

Adam looked to left and right as they crossed the road from the promenade. He ushered her inside and led the way through the door at the far end of the passage.

Ellie paused in pleasure on seeing the expanse of grass with tables and chairs scattered about in the shade. Birds sang in the sycamore tree in the corner. It looked idyllic.

'I found this the other day,' Adam said as he pulled out a chair for her 'They do delicious filled baguettes here at lunchtime. Or excellent toasted sandwiches if you prefer?'

They chose cheese and salad baguettes and lemonade shandy to drink.

'Now,' he said when they had been served.

There was a tiny pause. Ellie picked up her glass, took a sip and put it down again. The shandy was ice-cold and welcome.

'There seems to be a problem with Marsha,' he said at last. 'I understand the difficulties, of course, but by now certain things should in place and I'm afraid they're not.'

Ellie nodded. 'I agree with you.'

'All the publicity for both the music and art festivals has been already been dealt with from the London end, of course. The musicians asked to see to that themselves and they've got someone good in charge. The posters are already printed. So that's out of the way.'

'They're brilliant,' Ellie murmured. 'Eye-catching and informative. I've driven Miss Valence round the town to see them.'

'You're a kind girl.'

She felt her colour rise. 'All part of the job.'

'But the work for the art exhibition is not really in your brief?'

She shook her head. 'But I'm willing to give what help I can.' She didn't say that Marsha's attitude made this difficult but perhaps he guessed.

He took a bite of his baguette. 'More than perhaps you expected?'

'Something like that. But Miss Valence's welfare is in my brief. Not only that but I'm fond of her and I know how much the Culmore Pavilion means to her She's pinning such hopes on the opening and on the music festival especially. And of course the art exhibition is all tied up with that.' She wiped her mouth with the table napkin and marshalled her thoughts. She would have to take great care not to worry her employer with all this. 'So

92

what is it you want me to do?'

'I need to know if Marsha has assembled the list of exhibiting artists and the titles of their paintings so the exhibition brochure can be finalised. It's cutting it fine as it is and questions are being asked.'

She frowned. 'I understood that was well in hand.'

'Not as far as I know. And presumably the stewarding must be sorted out and a rota made. I was hoping to see Marsha this morning and ask to take a look at the file which hopefully contains the information we need. It's not over at the Culmore so must still be in her care.'

'I think it is. I know it's not in the office now unless Marsha's put it back there.' Ellie wrinkled her nose, trying to remember if she had seen it in Marsha's room yesterday evening. She was sure she hadn't.

'Could you get hold of it for me?'

'The office door was locked,' Ellie reminded him. 'We've never done that before and as far as I know there's only one key and it wasn't there.'

'It could be somewhere, else in her apartment.'

Ellie frowned in concentration. 'There should be a spare key somewhere among Miss Valence's papers. I'll see if I can locate it without her knowing why and asking questions.'

'Will that be a problem?'

'Hopefully not.'

'And if it doesn't turn up there? Would you be willing to search Marsha's room for it?'

She stared at him. 'You're asking me to raid her apartment?'

'Not raid, Ellie. Just a surface examination for the office key''

Put like that it didn't sound too bad.

He sank back in his seat, looking deflated. Ellie hated seeing him like this She wondered fleetingly if there was more to it than worry about Marsha's inability to take charge of the art side of things and that he was beginning to care for her. She took a deep breath and concentrated hard on suppressing the painful suspicion.

'I'll do my best to get it sorted out,' she said

'I know I can rely on you.'

Again she felt a flush of gratification and took another sip from her glass to cool down. 'I'll get back to you as soon as I can.'

'So I can report this afternoon that progress is being made? It's rather urgent. I have a meeting at the bank before that so time is pressing.'

'I know it's important, Adam.'

He nodded, draining his glass. 'Another?'

She shook her head. 'I must get back.'

'Thank you, Ellie,' he said and his brilliant smile gave her a surge of pleasure so great it was hard to breathe.

He was looking at her now as if there was something else he wanted to say but he got to his feet in silence. For a moment she hesitated. Then he indicated she should go before him across the grass, through the dimness of the building and then out into bright sunshine again. She was merely being fanciful to think there was more. The warmth of the day was getting to her and the beauty of that lovely garden.

'Good luck then, Ellie,' he said.

She smiled and his serious expression lifted a little.

It was only when he had left her to walk into town that it occurred to her that she was planning to do exactly what Ginette had suggested earlier just because Adam had asked her. Ginette would have a field day with that if she knew.

Ellie paused to consider this, leaning on the railings on the edge of the promenade and staring at the sea as if the waves breaking far out could tell her that this was the right thing to do in the circumstances and there was no need for her to feel guilty about it.

Did the end always justify the means? The result in this case would be the smooth running of the exhibition instead of chaos and confusion that would rebound on Adam because he was in overall charge. And Miss Valence would be happy, too. So, surely it must be right?

Below her the pebbles shone in the sunshine and the smell of seaweed on the rim of hard sand beyond wafted across to her. All at once her spirits lifted because Adam wanted her help and it was in her power to give it

'Hi, there!'

She turned, smiling at the speaker but not really seeing him because her mind was on Adam.

'Ellie, isn't it? Miss Valence's assistant, kind to old ladies like my dear mother and aunt?'

She blinked. Clad in shorts and T-shirt and carrying a vast hold-all, he seemed to radiate good health.

'Sorry to interrupt your reverie.'

'No, really. I'm just on my way back to Bredon Court.

'And I've just come from there checking on the Oldies.'

'You'd better not let them hear you calling them that. Especially your mother. David, isn't it?'

He bowed, his eyes dancing. 'David Lindle, new recruit at the sailing club and eager to fit in. I'll be moving down here permanently in a week or two. I'm just the occasional visitor from London until then.'

'And the hundredth new member of the sailing club?'

'Now, how did you know that?'

'I have spies.'

He laughed. 'The girl, Ginette?'

96

'The very one.'

'She's a character, isn't she? I wish I had her sailing expertise.'

'You're new to it, then?'

'Learning fast, I hope. Do you sail yourself?'

'Regretfully not. Too much to think about this summer with the festival coming up and the opening of the Culmore. Maybe next year.'

'Everyone's talking about the grand opening. I'm glad I'll be down for that. Mum and Aunt Barbara have bought new outfits for the preview evening so I hope they're on the invitation list?'

'I'm sure they are,' Ellie said. 'The invitations will be going out soon.' She crossed her fingers behind her back and tried to sound confident although she wasn't sure that Marsha had done anything about them yet. Something to check up on.

'I'll see you there, then, if not before. Meanwhile good luck.'

Ellie smiled and nodded. As she went on her way she thought he couldn't have wished her anything. She definitely needed luck with what she was planning to do.

She thought long and hard about obtaining the master keyring to the apartments without her employer asking why she wanted it.

With luck there was an office key on it although she hadn't noticed one there before. The obvious thing to do, of course, would be to ask Marsha, but since it seemed likely that she had locked the door deliberately this didn't seem a good idea.

Ellie and Ginette were sharing a quick coffee break seated on the low wall that bordered the patio in the back garden. Ellie gazed across the grass to her guinea pigs' hutch in the corner where overhanging branches gave them plenty of shade. Later she would put them out in their run, but for the moment she had more pressing things to consider.

'I reckon Wonder Girl has decided to move secretly into the Avalon Hotel so that her absence will worry poor Miss Valence to death and then she'll inherit everything,' Ginette said.

'Please don't joke about something so serious,' Ellie begged.

Ginette looked aggrieved. 'So you don't think there's a grain of truth in there somewhere?'

'It's not my place to think anything.'

'That's her devious plan for sure.'

'Half the time Miss Valence isn't aware of her absence so it's not going to work,' Ellie said.

'And neither is locking you out of the office,' Ginette said 'There's only one thing for it Get yourself into the apartment while she's out and have a snoop round.'

Elle sighed. 'I suppose.'

'A miracle might have happened,' Ginette said. 'The key might be back in the lock. How

98

will you know if you don't look?'

Ellie drank the last of her coffee and sprang up. 'You're right.'

She felt in her pocket for the apartment key as she went through the hall, tapped on the door of Marsha's apartment to check that she wasn't there, and went in. So far so good. No need to panic. A quick glance at the office door showed her that the key wasn't there.

Ellie had expected this but still felt dismay because,she was about to enter someone else's domain without permission. It was strangely difficult to open the door into the sitting-room that so recently been hers. The furniture was still arranged in the same way, but a vase of scented cream lilies stood on the sideboard and gave an exotic feel to the place that hadn't been there before.

Ellie froze at the sound of a turning key in the lock of the front door of the apartment. Heart thudding, she slipped quickly back into the hallway just as the door opened. Everything seemed to be happening in slow motion, Marsha nudging it wide open with her shoulder and coming awkwardly in. One of her crutches scraped the wall and she gave an exclamation of annoyance before slamming the door shut with one arm.

Marsha didn't see her immediately and Ellie had time to compose her expression in to one of pleased surprise at seeing her before giving a greeting in a voice she tried hard to keep steady.

'Ellie Langley?' Marsha paused and leaned on her crutches. 'No use trying to get into the office. What do you want anyway? Don't say that my great-aunt is checking up on me again and sent you here to spy?'

'I . . I needed to see you.'

Ellie stood aside for Marsha to get past, hoping to keep up the appearance of nonchalance. To stop her hands trembling she clenched them at her side.

'You'd better come in then.'

This time the scent of the lilies was overwhelming. The horror of being discovered rummaging through Marsha's belongings if the interruption had come a little later was beginning to get to her. Thank goodness she had been spared that Ellie thought. But now more quick thinking on her part was needed.

'The personal invitations to the festival preview evening,' she said, her voice trembling a little. 'Would you like me to help you with them?'

'So kind. I've been working something out I'll show you. But first let's have a drink.'

Taken aback, Ellie sank down on the seat indicated while Marsha poured two glasses of red wine from the bottle on the table. At once Ellie sprang up again to carry them across for her. Nodding her thanks, Marsha seated herself in a large armchair and smiled pleasantly.

'Now, Ellie, tell me all about yourself,' she said.

This was eerie. Ellie looked at Marsha in suspicion and caught a gleam of malice in her eyes although her lips were curved into a smile.

'I like working for your great-aunt,' she blurted out. 'I'm fond of her ' She took a large gulp of wine, swallowed it too quickly and then had a spasm of coughing.

'Too strong for you?' Marsha asked with obvious pleasure.

This was the Marsha she had come to know, Ellie thought, and the incentive she needed not to be taken in by the apparent friendliness. 'Sorry about that.' She took another sip of wine. 'This is kind of you, Marsha. And now I'd like to do something to help.'

Marsha's eyes narrowed. 'The invitations are all in hand, I assure you. I'll show you what I've drafted out.'

She heaved herself out of her chair and with the aid of her crutches moved across to the writing desk in the corner. 'Here,' she said, handing Ellie a sheet of paper.

The handwriting was small and neat. Ellie read quickly, impressed by the way Marsha had worded the invitation with all the relevant information set out clearly. It professed to come from Miss Valence and her name was written in bold type at the top.

'I shall insist on a good quality card,'

Marsha said 'Deckle-edged. What are your thoughts on colour? I think my great-aunt would like cream. Tasteful, you see, and fitting to the occasion.'

Ellie agreed, surprised that Marsha seemed anxious to please Miss Valence who would be delighted at the compliment. She banished the brief thought that if something seemed too good to be true if probably was 'This is great,' Ellie said 'Would you like me to type it up for you?'

'Of course. The key to your office is on the ledge above the door for safe keeping. And then type the addresses where they have to go. There's a list there and pile of envelopes. The printers can get them out at once. And when you've done it you can organise a taxi for me. I shall visit the printers myself.'

'Shall I do it for you?'

Marsha frowned. 'You think I'm not capable?'

Enough said. A quick phone call to her employer to say what she was doing set her mind at rest and Ellie set to work. The file was back in the office to be examined when she wished and she knew where the key was kept. Problem solved.

'That's all,' Marsha said in a dismissive tone of voice when Ellie had finished.

Ellie couldn't wait to tell Ginette. As soon as she had made a copy of the list for herself, phoned for a taxi and replaced the office key in its new home she went to find her, exultant at the ease all this had been accomplished.

Treachery Occurs

Ellie found Adam on the balcony leaning on the balustrade and gazing out to sea at the white sails of a dinghy heeling in the breeze. Nearby a couple of gulls quarrelled and then flew off with shrill cries.

'You've caught me taking a few moments' rest in a heavy schedule,' he said as she approached. 'Good news, I hope?'

'The best,' she told him, smiling. 'I came at once to tell you. The missing file is now safely in my apartment. I'll study it carefully and make sure that I complete everything for the art exhibition that still needs to be done. The festival committee are still happy about providing the wine?'

'And nibbles,' he said, smiling. 'So now you can relax, Ellie,' he said. 'And so can I, I've been feeling more than a little guilty involving you in something so unorthodox when you obviously hated the idea. You coped well.'

She felt herself flush at his praise.

'My business went well this morning, too,' he added. 'Have we time for a celebratory drink, do you think?'

'Why not. As long as long as mine can be elderflower cordial?'

103

'Good idea,' he said 'A clear head. I'll join you in that.'

From where they stood on the balcony they had a good view of the dinghy coming back to shore and for a few moments they watched, sipping their drinks, as the boat was beached and the sails came down.

Ellie was glad to be here with Adam for these few precious moments. The sunlight reflecting from the window glass behind him seemed to give his tanned face and neck a special glow. She hoped it did the same for her even though she made sure to keep out of the hot sun when she could.

'I like to see those boats out there on the water,' he said. 'There's something appealing about being part of the elements whatever the weather.'

'I might even have a go myself,' Ellie said 'I can understand the joy of it now.'

'Do you think you will?'

She smiled. 'I'll think about it.'

The short silence between them seemed uneasy for no apparent reason. Then Adam cleared his throat.

'The officials of the sailing club tell me that they run special classes for beginners,' he said at last. 'They like to encourage participation in all aspects of the club. I like that.' He looked thoughtfully down at the glass in his hand and then up again. 'We've been discussing donating a trophy for the winner of the big race on the eve of the opening of the festival. The Culmore Trophy.'

'That sounds good,' she said

'You approve?'

'It's a brilliant idea. It'll connect the Culmore with other events of the town in a good sort of way. I'm all for that.'

He nodded. 'I'd like us like to sponsor a club boat as well in due course. It would be a good opportunity to get more young people involved in such a healthy activity. Not everyone can own their own boats.'

'I like the idea of that, too.'

He downed his drink. 'I must be off.'

She knew this brief interlude must soon end. They were busy people and Adam had the festival committee meeting this afternoon. He would be able to tell them now that the invitations would soon be sent out.

His mobile rang.

She stepped to one side while he answered its 'Marsha?' he said 'Yes, of course. I'll be right along.' He clicked it off and turned to Ellie, frowning. 'Marsha's here.'

She nodded, biting her lip. Marsha, having done her bit at the printers would have come to put Adam in the picture. What was more natural than that?

Deep in thought, Adam pocketed his mobile and indicated that Ellie should go ahead of him into the building. He smiled at her as they walked together towards his office, but she knew he didn't welcome this visit any more than she did.

Marsha was waiting near the main door, leaning on her crutches. The expression on her face was stony as she saw Ellie with Adam.

'Marsha!' Adam said, moving quickly towards her.

'I must go;' Ellie said, holding back a little.

Marsha looked her up and down. 'I think you better had,' she said in a voice deep with suspicion. 'For someone who is supposed to be P.A. to my poor great-aunt you seem to be doing very little assisting.'

'Instead she's assisting you,' Adam said pleasantly.

'Oh?' Marsha said She gazed up at Adam as if anxious to know how that could possibly be.

'I understand that she's at hand to help you with anything that needs doing in a practical way.'

'Even if it means neglecting my great-aunt?'

'You won't find Ellie doing that,' Adam said with confidence.

Adam was made of sterner stuff than she was, Ellie thought. All she could do was flush and look guilty when there was not any need for that at all.

'Thanks, Ellie,' Adam said 'I'll be in touch.'

Ellie nodded and went out into the chilly wind that seemed to have sprung up from nowhere.

When Marsha left after a lengthy session

with him at the bar, Adam went straight to his office and sank down on the chair at his desk. What a girl . . . acting as if her clumsy gait on her crutches was merely a minor inconvenience instead of holding her back from enjoying herself doing what she wanted to do.

He was still convinced that organising the art exhibition was not that and never had been Maybe her great-aunt had forced it on her for reasons of her own. Could be she wanted to see more of her great-niece and this was one way of doing so?

He knew only too well the strength of Miss Valence's character when she decided on a course of action. From the first he had seen something of that determination in Marsha, too, so maybe he was wrong about that.

In the bar they hadn't spoken of the arrangements for the opening that was forefront in his mind, but of the musicians who would soon be descending on Cheselton-on-Sea and might need entertaining.

Marsha's eyes had lit up and the attractive dimple in her cheeks came and went as she outlined some ideas of her own. Now that Ellie had gone Marsha seemed to relax and become truly entertaining. He found he was enjoying himself even though he should be back in his office working hard.

He was proud of parting with Ellie so casually as if it didn't matter in the least to him. Her fiancé was a lucky man. He had caught glimpses of her in the company of a fair-haired chap once or twice. The girl who cleaned the apartments at Bredon Court had been there, too, laughing and joking. Ellie seemed to have many friends. He hoped she considered him one of them, too.

He smiled as he thought of her pleasure when he told her of his plan to present the trophy to the sailing club. He had chosen the design of the trophy with care and the committee had approved whole-heartedly. He could honestly say that his belief that one of the sailors meant a great deal to her had nothing at all to do with his suggestion of the trophy to the committee.

He busied himself now putting everything on his desk in order, placing a pile of papers neatly in one corner and sliding some others inside the top drawer. That done to his satisfaction he glanced at his watch. Time to get a bite to eat before assembling his notes for the meeting at two o'clock.

*   *   *

Ellie spent the rest of the day examining the information file that she had removed from Marsha's apartment.

She took an hour typing the list of paintings and artists with their exhibiting numbers so she could assemble a catalogue for visitors to the art exhibition. When that was completed she turned her attention to the stewarding rota.

The application forms were all there in the file, which made things easier because each exhibitor had been asked to indicate which days they were free to be on stewardship duty at the exhibition. A few phone calls to check and the job was done.

When consulted, Miss Valence was helpful in suggesting someone with perfect handwriting who would be willing to write out the display cards to be placed alongside each exhibit. Ellie, checking by phone from her employer's apartment, soon had this organised. She would take the list round early next day.

The glow of a job well done was wonderful.

'So now everything is in order for the grand opening of the Culmore Pavilion and for the preview evening?' Miss Valence said.

'I believe it is,' Ellie said. 'For the preview anyway, and I'm sure Adam will have it all in hand.'

'And Marsha will be pleased.'

'I hope so.'

Miss Valence looked at her kindly 'I'm well aware of your input for the art exhibition, Ellie, my dear,' she said 'And I'm grateful. Marsha has had so much to contend with. She needed you and I'm glad you felt able to help.'

Ellie was touched. 'I know how much the Culmore means to you,' she said 'Your grandfather would have been so proud.'

'I think so, too, my dear. And now I'd like another look at my album if you would be so kind. And you, Ellie, must take some fresh air. You deserve some time to yourself.'

There was no better way to do this than by taking Daisy out for an evening walk, Ellie thought as she ran upstairs for her jacket. Coming down again she heard the door on the first landing crash shut as Marjorie Lindle's son, David, came lumbering out, laden with a hold-all, sailing anorak and life jacket.

'Ellie,' he said with evident pleasure.

She smiled. 'David.'

He cleared his throat and then hesitated as if he didn't quite know what to say.

She looked at him encouragingly 'So you've joined the sailing club?'

'How did you know?' He moved his hold-all from one arm to the other.

'Not difficult,' she said, eyeing it.

'Oh, I see.' A faint pink tinged his cheeks. 'My Aunt Barbara was just talking about you She thinks you look exhausted with all the extra work foisted on you.'

'Could be. But how does she know that?'

'An eye for detail, my aunt,' he said.

That was true, Ellie thought. Barbara Whitlock had an air about her that always gave the impression she was watching every move.

'Is everything all right with them both? she asked. 'I'm surprised to see you here

110

midweek?'

'They're fine, thanks. I took the day off so I could come down. I can't keep away.'

'So the sailing bug's got to you?'

'Something like that.' He smiled and at once looked more confident. 'You wouldn't feel like coming along to watch?'

'Why not? I'd like that.' Daisy wouldn't mind relinquishing an extra walk, especially as she didn't know anything about it.

'You would?' he sounded surprised, but pleased, too.

He strode along the seafront and Ellie had to run to keep up with him. Good exercise, she told herself, and just what she needed. Barbara Whitlock was right in her summing up of the situation. Maybe she would also know how long Marsha was spending with Adam over at the Culmore.

'Something amusing you?' David said, glancing at her sideways.

'Do you think your aunt would make a good fortune teller?'

'Undoubtedly.'

She smiled. 'Has she told yours?'

'She warned me to steer clear of her landlady's great-niece. Not so easy, though, when the great-niece makes a play for you in the local hostelry.'

'Marsha spends time there?' Ellie asked, surprised.

'Not any more apparently. She has her eyes

on bigger game now, according to my aunt. Out for the kill.'

Ellie laughed, but she wished she hadn't asked.

They arrived at the sailing club where several boats were being prepared for the evening race. Ellie expected that David would suggest she kept out of the way and watched the proceedings from the gallery, but to her surprise he wanted her help with removing the canvas cover of the boat he would be crewing in because the helmsman would be arriving late.

Ignoring Ginette's shrieks of surprise on seeing her, Ellie concentrated on the instructions David was giving her. Under his supervision Ellie climbed inside the boat and held the mast in position while he fixed what needed to be done.

'Excellent,' he said as she climbed out again. 'I owe you, Ellie. Would you be willing to join me at the bar after the race?'

She was glad to agree because he was so grateful and felt carefree for the first time in days. It must be something to do with the happy atmosphere here in the boat yard, she thought.

*　　　*　　　*

Daisy's morning walk along the sea front a day or two later was earlier than usual, because Ellie wanted to do some shopping for Amanda's birthday at the end of August before taking her employer's breakfast into her at nine o'clock. She had seen a beautiful cream leather-bound photograph album in the window of the newsagents that opened early and wanted to buy it before anyone else had the same idea. Her step-mother always printed out loads of photographs from her digital camera. She would love this.

Outside Bredon Court Ellie smiled at the postman on his early Saturday round and then went in herself to return Daisy to her owner.

Mrs Drew had changed out of the dressing gown she was wearing earlier and now wore the brown outfit she kept for weekends. She looked strangely upset.

'My cousin's going to be disappointed,' she said as she took Daisy's lead. 'She planned to escort me to the opening and art preview thing at the Culmore, but now the time's been changed she'll be at work.'

Ellie looked at her in surprise. 'The time's changed and the day?'

'Didn't you know? Here, I'll show you. Come inside.' Mrs Drew released Daisy who shook herself vigorously and bounded off in search of food.

Mrs Drew picked up the invitation from the window-sill and handed it to Ellie.

'There! It's only just come.'

Ellie stared down at the cream deckle-edged

card chosen to please Miss Valence and read with amazement the words on it embossed in dark blue. These weren't the same she had typed out from Marsha's handwriting a day or two ago. She read them again to make sure.

Daisy's slurping of her food in the kitchen was the only sound in a silence that seemed to last for ever.

'This is wrong,' Ellie said at last. She felt cold. They would all be incorrect, all the invitations sent to the dignitaries of the town and people of the music world as well as *Friends of the Culmore*. She couldn't begin to imagine how this mistake could have happened.

'May I borrow this?' she said. 'I need to look into it.'

'Keep it,' Mrs Drew said 'It's no use to me. I won't enjoy it without Jane.'

She sounded so despondent Ellie wished she could change the wording on the card instantly.

'With luck you won't have to,' she said. 'I'll do the best I can, Mrs Drew. And thanks for pointing it out.'

She closed Mrs Drew's door and at the same time the opposite one opened and Marsha emerged in a smart jacket and long skirt.

'You can tell my aunt I'll be in touch with her when I get back,' she said as she manoeuvred herself out on her crutches.

Ellie watched her go in silence. The

114

implications of the mistake were getting to her now with a numbing feeling of shock. Because of it she had let Marsha go without saying anything. What a fool!

She had to think. She had typed the correct date and time, she was sure of it. So what could have gone wrong?

She served her employer's breakfast in a daze, replying to everything she said without remembering much about it afterwards. The thought uppermost in her mind was that she hadn't bought Amanda's birthday present. As if that mattered at a time of crisis like this when her birthday was some weeks away.

'Are you well, Ellie?' Miss Valence asked as Ellie poured her another cup of tea. 'You don't seem quite yourself this morning.'

'There's something I need to do.'

'Of course, my dear. Go ahead by all means. I shall linger over my breakfast. There's no hurry.'

'I won't be long.'

Out on the pavement Ellie stood irresolute while the Saturday morning traffic thundered past. She glanced across at the Culmore Pavilion disappointed not to see Adam's car already there. The morning sunlight brightened the building and the background of sea sparkled as if this was an ordinary day and nothing much was amiss.

She thought of Adam's likely reaction to this latest problem. What would he do? She

115

had pushed Mrs Drew's invitation into her pocket and now she got it out and looked at it again. Although she was sure she wasn't to blame she needed to check that the mistake wasn't hers.

Moments later she was back inside and unlocking the door to Marsha's apartment, relieved to find that the key to the office door was in its hiding place. She ran her fingers along the edge of the desk as she waited for the computer to do its bit so she could get into the file she had saved. And there on the screen were the words she had typed exactly as she had typed them. She had already saved them on memory stick so there was no need to do it again.

Afterwards she wondered at the calm way she printed out the page and folded it to put in her pocket. Then she came out of the programme and switched off the computer. All the time she was doing this her mind raged at Marsha's treachery, for it could only have been Marsha's doing.

The invitations had been posted to arrive today, Saturday, when the local printers were closed. That much was certain. And it was deliberate. But why had Marsha done it? Incredible to believe she had planned to jeopardise the opening ceremony and preview of the art exhibition when she was nominally in charge. Could it be that she planned to phone round everybody to put the matter right, implying that Miss Valence herself had been at fault and could no longer cope? Ellie wouldn't believe this of anyone else. But Marsha? Could be. Out on the pavement again Ellie looked across at the empty car park at the Culmore Pavilion. In the other direction a lot of activity was going on at the sailing club and already two boats were out on the water. Since her imagination about it was in overdrive she longed, suddenly, to hear Ginette's take on this latest development.

She found her in the boatyard in her bulky sailing gear in animated conversation with Sam, also dressed in blue anorak and orange buoyancy aid.

They turned as she called to them.

'Something wrong, Ellie?' Ginette asked in concern. 'You look dreadful.'

She pulled out the paper with the correct wording to show them.

'Thursday afternoon for the art preview and the meet the musicians event, when by rights it should be Friday evening after the opening ceremony?' Sam said. 'But can't you just explain the mistake to everyone?'

'Have some sense,' Ginette retorted. 'You can't mess people about like that. You have to be professional.'

Sam frowned, obviously deep in thought.

'Suppose the people invited don't get the revised date for some reason or other. Imagine all the big-wigs from far and wide arriving in their finery a day too early, no food laid on, the art exhibition not ready, the musicians and their families still on the way here. Bedlam.'

'But they'll surely know the correct date by then.'

'And they'll already have made arrangements to take time off work on Thursday afternoon. They won't like it. They'll want to blame someone. Miss Valence, most likely, as her name's on them. And suppose the local paper gets to hear about it?'

'I see what you mean,' he said slowly.

'So what are we going to do?' Ginette demanded.

Suddenly Sam brightened. 'Paper and pen?'

'What use is that?'

He unzipped his buoyancy aid. 'Get some Ginette, and don't waste time arguing. We'll need to draft out an apology on the way there.' He was out of his sailing jacket now. 'Get a move on.'

Ginette was off at once, shouting to David to explain what had happened and shedding her sailing clothes as she went.

Bemused, Ellie stared after her. She felt lightheaded at the speed Sam was taking charge. At the same time she was aware that Adam was on the balcony at the Culmore looking in their direction.

The next moment a wave of dizziness swept over her and only Sam's arms round her prevented her falling to the ground.

118

Cruel Sabotage

'All right, Ellie?' Sam asked, his voice anxious. She struggled for control but was glad to lean against him for a minute or two.

'I'm fine now,' she said at last. 'Thanks, Sam.'

He released her and she stood up straight to prove that her dizziness had passed now. She glanced towards the Culmore and saw that Adam had gone now. She took several deep breaths of breezy air while Sam tapped in a number on his mobile and spoke urgently.

Ginette was back. She held out a biro and a red-covered pad.

'Come on,' Sam said. 'My car's over there.'

Minutes later they were fastening their seat belts and Sam dictating a letter of apology and Ginette scribbling his words down.

'Where are we going?' Ellie asked as they set off.

'The printers,' he said.

'But they're closed on Saturdays.'

'Not for me. Not today. This is an emergency. Andy Rice will meet us there. Between us we'll reprint the invitations and the letters. Then we'll get the local ones delivered by hand, work something out about the others later. Fancy a long car ride about the countryside, Ginette?'

119

His voice rang with confidence. Ellie had forgotten that Sam worked at Hackett and. Blunt's. She leaned back and closed her eyes, thankful that something was being done to set things straight.

It was good to let Sam take charge.

Only later, when the printing was done, and Sam and Ginette had set off on a delivery route involving many miles of driving, did she remember the sailing race they were preparing for when she ran across to tell them of Marsha's latest game. They had given that up without a moment's hesitation.

Her eyes filled with tears at their generosity and she didn't at first see David waiting for her on a seat on the promenade opposite Bredon Court.

He crossed the road to join her.

'Crisis over?' he said.

'You knew about it?'

'Ginette yelled something as she rushed past. I couldn't let Brian down by not crewing for him or I'd have helped, too.'

'You're so kind,' she said, a lump in her throat.

He flushed and moved his weight froth one foot to the other. 'I wonder . . . would it help to talk about it?'

She nodded.

'Coffee somewhere close?'

'That would be good, but I mustn't be long.'

She was still clutching the pile of invitations

it was her job to deliver in the town as well as those due to be posted to the *Friends of the Culmore* who lived too far away to be delivered by hand.

David eyed them as they seated themselves in a corner table at the cafe on the corner. 'I'll help you with those if you like.'

'Some are local ones I'm to deliver,' Ellie said. 'I'll get the London ones in the post for Monday. It's too late for them to go today.'

'No need,' he said. 'I'll sort that lot out for you when I get back tomorrow.'

'Would you?'

'It wouldn't be any problem.' The anxious expression in his eyes deepened.

'That's really kind.'

'I've got a condition, though. Would you see that one of them goes to Mum and my aunt? My life wouldn't be worth living if they don't get one. Can't you just imagine Aunt Barbara stamping about in a temper and Mum exercising more furiously and pretending not to mind?'

She giggled and he laughed, too, as he went to the counter to collect their coffee.

'Will you be able to be there at opening, David?'

He looked at her and smiled. 'I could get down early on Friday evening, I suppose. Would you like that?'

'Only if you would.'

Ellie moved a little in her chair, afraid

121

of something intangible in the air. But she admonished herself for imagining things. She smiled. 'I think your mother and aunt would like you to be there.'

Confiding in David felt good and she was happier about it all by the time they got up to go. She had divided the invitations into two piles. When she had delivered hers she would take one over to the Culmore for Adam's files. With luck it wouldn't have occurred to Marsha to do that and so he wouldn't have seen the wrong one. First, though, she had some explaining to do to her employer because she had left her enjoying a leisurely breakfast with the promise she would be back very soon. And that was hours ago, or so it seemed.

She found Miss Valence slumped forward in her chair by the window and for a moment, stunned, she gazed at her unable to move further in to the room. Then her employer moved slightly, murmuring something Ellie couldn't hear.

She rushed forward and threw herself down on her knees at her side. 'You're ill and I wasn't here to help,' she cried.

Miss Valence opened her eyes and tried to sit up.

'No, don't move,' Ellie said urgently. 'Wait just a minute. I'll get some water.'

She held the glass to her lips and had a napkin ready in case of spills. After a while faint colour appeared in her employer's cheeks and she was able, with Ellie's help, to move herself into a sitting position.

'What happened? Can you tell me?' Ellie said.

The phone rang before Miss Valence could answer.

'David Lindle,' a voice said when Ellie lifted the receiver.

'David Lindle?' she repeated, bemused.

'The chap you had coffee with a short while ago.'

'Oh yes. David. Sorry.'

'Are you OK, Ellie? You sound odd.'

'It's Miss Valence. She's unwell. I've just found her. I think she passed out . .'

'I'll be right there.'

He was with them in minutes and took in the situation at a glance. 'Best phone for an ambulance,' he said with such authority that Ellie didn't hesitate.

'They won't be long,' she said as she replaced the receiver. 'I'll need to get some of her things ready to take with her.'

He nodded and seated himself on a chair at Miss Valence's side. When she returned he was holding her hand and leaning towards her. A big man, he towered over her and Ellie saw a likeness to his aunt, Barbara Whitlock, as he heard her return with Miss Valence's belongings.

He looked up. 'All set?'

She nodded. She was lucky he could come.

His support was comforting when she needed it.

*   *   *

'So she's staying in hospital for one night at least?' Ginette said, round-eyed. 'Poor lady. She'll hate that. How did you get back just now?'

'David was wonderful. He stayed with me all the time I was there and drove me back again afterwards.'

Suddenly overcome Ellie sank down in her employer's armchair and leaned forward with her head in her hands. 'I should have been with her when it happened,' she said.

'Have some sense, Ellie,' Ginette said. 'What could you have done if you'd been on duty? More than likely you'd have been downstairs in the office beavering away or running in circles round Wonder Girl.'

'Marsha!' Ellie said, sitting up right. 'She'll need to know about this.' She sprang to her feet.

'She's not in,' Ginette pointed out.

'I'll leave a message on her answer phone.'

'She'll take no notice,' Ginette said with scorn.

Ignoring her Ellie left her message and replaced the receiver.

'You pander to her.'

'She has to know. She's her next of kin.'

124

Ellie stared at Ginette in horror. 'That sounds awful.'

'Sensible not awful. How was Miss Valence when you left her?'

'Pale and a bit shaky. She seems to approve of David.'

'Anyone would approve of him. I do myself.'

Ellie smiled but then was solemn again as she busied herself taking the cloth off the table. 'It's strange, Ginette,' she said. 'Miss Valence doesn't want Adam to visit her. I don't know why. Somehow I'll have to prevent his showing up at the hospital.'

'I'll pop in to see her before the evening race,' Ginette said. 'And if I'm banned, too, I'll take no notice.'

*   *   *

Ellie knocked on the closed door of Adam's office at the Culmore Pavilion in the hope she would find him there. She knew he had been working late these past few evenings.

'Come in!'

She opened the door, the revised invitation in her hand.

He got up as he saw her. 'Ellie?'

'I've come to give you this for your records,' she said. 'And also to tell you that Miss Valence is in hospital. She had more or less collapsed when I found her.'

He looked shocked. 'And now?'

'Looking a little better,' she said 'That's all I know.'

'Here, sit down, Ellie. Tell me what happened?'

His voice was deeply reassuring and she found it easy to pour out her concern for her employer and her remorse that she wasn't with her when Miss Valence started to feel. By the time she had finished even she could tell it was nonsense to think that her presence would have made any difference.

He glanced at his watch. 'What are the visiting hours? Is there time for me to call in and see her now?'

She shook her head. 'Please, not for the moment, Adam. Tomorrow, perhaps. I'll let you know if she can have visitors.'

'Very well.'

She was relieved that he accepted it without question. She passed it across the invitation she was holding.

'Is this for me? What is it?' He opened it But I've got one of these already.'

'Not like this.'

He looked at her sharply.

'Something was wrong with the wording,' she said.

'Are you all right, Ellie? I thought I saw you earlier looking unwell. It was you, wasn't it, in that man's arms?'

For a moment she was startled and then she remembered. 'It was nothing,' she said. 'I was

126

lucky Sam was there to catch me. I'm OK now that this mistake's been sorted out.'

'But how did you come to make such a mistake in the first place?'

She hesitated. Adam was frowning at her, obviously suspicious. Surely he didn't think her mind was on other things so she was unable to concentrate?

'It wasn't like that,' she said 'I can't say more A reprint's been done and the replacement invitations delivered by hand, most of them.'

'By *your* hand?'

She shook her head. 'Mostly by Ginette and her friend. David's taking the London ones back with him tomorrow. He'll see they're delivered.'

'David?'

'Someone at the sailing club.'

'I see. Am I right in suspecting Marsha's behind this?'

Ellie hesitated again.

'It can't go on,' he said, his voice sharp. 'Ignoring her duties is one thing but making such an elementary mistake in the invitations is not on. I'll get across there now and have it out with her.'

'No!' Ellie had tried Marsha's apartment again. Since she had found no-one there she had left a note in a prominent position, hoping Marsha would be back soon and see it. A row between her and Adam at this moment would not be a good thing.

He sat down on his chair again.

'You're right of course, Ellie,' he said 'Marsha will be at the hospital now with her great-aunt.'

'Could you leave this to me, Adam?' she said 'Everything about the invitations is in place now and the problem solved. I'll let you know about the visiting.'

He nodded. 'Very well. And Ellie, try not to worry too much. There's help here if you need it.'

She knew that of course, but it was good to hear Adam put it into words.

She would have liked nothing better at the moment than to be sure that Marsha had got her message and was even now at her great-aunt's bedside showing concern for her welfare. But she had little hope of that.

Ginette was there with Miss Valence when Ellie arrived at the hospital and left immediately, signalling to Ellie with an expressive shrug of her shoulders that no-one else had been in and certainly not Marsha.

Ellie sat down in her vacated chair, prepared to stay as long as she was allowed.

*   *   *

She was feeding her guinea pigs when she heard the sound of a car drawing-up outside Bredon Court and knew that Marsha had returned. She crossed the dusky lawn knowing

128

she had a difficult task ahead of her. Telling Marsha face-to-face about her great-aunt was much better than her reading it in a note stuck to her door.

But she wasn't quite quick enough.

Surprised to see her inside the building already, Ellie hesitated as Marsha tore the note off and swung round on her crutches to face her. Her cheeks were flushed and her eyes bright.

'So what's this? Don't tell me my great-aunt has succumbed at last!' Her voice had a triumphant ring to it that sent a chill through Ellie. She had a swift vision of Dad and Amanda standing in the entrance hall and Marsha surveying her surroundings as if she already owned them.

'I've been trying to get hold of you, Marsha.'

'What for? She's in hospital, isn't she? What better place?' Her words sounded caring, Ellie thought, if you didn't suspect her motives.

'They can't tell us much at the moment,' she said coldly. 'The doctor will be seeing her again in the morning.'

'I shan't hold my breath.'

'They said to phone about eleven.'

Marsha shrugged. 'So you can do that, can't you?'

'But you're her next of kin.'

'Don't let that stop you any more than it has already.' Marsha's eyes sparkled. 'Hospital's the best place for an old woman like her. I think you should start making enquiries about nursing homes that would be glad to take her You'll have plenty of free time now, won't you, until a decision is made? And we shan't be needing you after that.'

Ellie, speechless, watched her unlock the door and get herself inside the apartment.

*   *   *

Phone the person in charge of setting up the screens in the exhibition room to check that all was in order for Thursday.

Check that the caterers had everything in hand for Friday evening.

Type out a rota chart for the stewards to be fixed to the table where they would sit'

Check on the supply of bubble wrap, paper clips, extra labels and all the paraphernalia that might be required each day of the exhibition.

All these tasks helped keep Ellie's mind occupied next morning until it was time to phone the hospital.

Ginette was with her and Ellie was glad of her company. She hadn't told her of Marsha's joyful reaction on learning about her great-aunt because it was too painful to think about. Instead she busied herself making cups of coffee until it was time to pick up the phone.

Ginette's eyes looked anxious.

'And so?' she demanded. 'How is she?'

'She had a comfortable night. They have

130

some tests lined up but they didn't say much more than that. I can go in later this morning.'

'That's good, isn't it? Let's have another coffee to celebrate.'

Ellie smiled. 'You're joking, I'm swimming in it.'

'Me, too, if I'm honest. And I've work to do.' Ginette got up and stretched her bare arms above her head. 'I'll spread the word around. All the tenants will be concerned about her.'

Except for Marsha, Ellie thought sadly.

*　　　*　　　*

'Ellie!' Miss Valence said with pleasure as Ellie entered the sideward. 'How nice of you to come. Are those roses for me? Thank you, my dear.'

She was looking a little less pale today, Ellie noticed, but she seemed to have shrunk as she lay there beneath the cream bed cover. She placed the flowers on the locker and kissed her lightly on the forehead.

'Everyone sends their love. Adam, too,' she said.

Her employer looked alarmed. 'He's not coming to see me?'

'I said we'd let him know about visiting.'

'He's a busy man. And Marsha has a lot to do, too, and it's awkward with her broken ankle. So I thought it would be best.'

131

Her voice trailed away and Ellie hastened to reassure her. After that she answered her questions abut the programme for the re-opening of the Culmore Pavilion on Friday evening.

'And we're banking on your being there, too,' Ellie said.

'Yes, my dear, I mean to be there,' Miss Valence said, smiling. 'I'll have a few strong words to say to the doctor.'

Ellie smiled, too. He wouldn't stand a chance against her employer, she thought. At least she hoped not.

A stir in the doorway alerted them to more visitors. Ellie swung round to see Marsha manoeuvring herself in through the door that was held open by Adam.

She stared at him in dismay 'Adam!'

A flicker of surprise crossed his face as she got to her feet. He gave a small awkward shrug.

'Marsha, my dear girl!' Miss Valence said, raising herself on her pillow. 'And Adam, too.'

Her employer's smile was so genuine that Ellie had no doubt of her pleasure in seeing them together even though she had been adamant a little while ago that she didn't want Adam to come.

'Dear Aunt Lola, I was so worried about you,' Marsha said, smiling. 'Adam's been so kind.' She glanced at Ellie and away again. 'And attentive, too. He insisted on bringing me to see you in the hospital straight away and so here we are.' She looked round for somewhere to put her crutches.

Ellie indicated her empty chair and Adam pulled forward another. But before Ellie could sit down again a strict voice from the doorway made her pause.

'Only two visitors allowed per patient, if you please.'

So that was that. Ellie said a quick goodbye to the patient and left. Her last sight of them was of Marsha, in her pretty pink dress, gazing up at Adam with a proprietary air while Miss Valence looked on, smiling.

* * *

Adam had been pleased to see Miss Valence's delight as she smiled at her great-niece who had taken the trouble to come and see her. Not a great deal of trouble on Marsha's part, as it happened, because he was in the right place at the right time and all Marsha had to do was indicate that she wished to go to the hospital, but for some reason was unable to order a taxi immediately.

Standing by his car in the car park he had been feeling a sense of excitement at his decision to apply for the permanent position of Manager of Culmore. He liked Cheselton and would be happy to make his home here for the foreseeable future. An important part of the job would be arranging concerts throughout the year and having the opportunity to play the saxophone again when his hand was healed.

So, standing there, he was a sitting duck for Marsha, he thought. He could do little else than to fall in with her request, but he wished that Ellie had been free to take her instead of being involved with her fiancé as Marsha had been quick to tell him. She wasn't criticising Ellie in the least, she hastened to assure him. Ellie was due some time off and what better way to spend it?

But he was aware of Marsha's calculating air as he helped her into his car and took her crutches from her

They didn't stay long at the hospital and as he stood up to go Miss Valence pressed his hand. 'You'll look after her, won't you?' she murmured.

'Of course,' he had said.

Afterwards he had wondered about that. He had assumed at the time that she was referring the drive back to Bredon Court.

He smiled wryly as he helped Marsha out of the car, holding her crutches ready and making sure she was steady as she took them.

'I have a bottle of *Chateauneuf du Pape* opened and ready for our return,' she told him. 'You'll join me, of course, Adam.'

It sounded like a command, but he didn't feel the need to fall in with her wishes in this instance.

'Well, no, I'm afraid not, delightful as it
134

sounds.'

She eyed him suspiciously 'Not another engagement?'

'Pressure of work, Marsha. I'm sorry. You know how it is with all the organising still to be done.'

His reason was genuine and he hoped his refusal sounded suitably regretful. A glance of annoyance from those pretty eyes of hers was enough to make him glad he had made it, even though now he felt- churlish at having done so. He needed lunch anyway and it wouldn't have cost him much of his time to have suggested sharing a sandwich or two with her at the place he frequented along the front.

He went back to his office at the Culmore feeling disgruntled for no good reason. His hard work must be getting to him more than he realised.

*　　　*　　　*

Ellie had viewed Beachy Head often enough from a distance, but now she decided to drive there even though it was at least fifteen miles away. She had an urge to be out of doors somewhere high up. She longed as well to feel the downland air on her face and smell the sweet-flowered turf beneath her feet.

She bought a packet of cheese sandwiches from a kiosk on the way and, when she got to her destination, parked her car near three others. Then she walked to the highest point-where she could look over at the steep cliff and marvel at the way the sunshine highlighted certain obtruding patches into dazzling white.

Before taking a path along the top of the chalky cliffs she stood for a moment, breathing deeply and feeling the peace seeping into her body.

She began to walk, following the undulating cliff path for some distance before finding a grassy bank dotted with daisies that made a fine seat. She ate slowly, relishing the warmth on her face, and enjoying the freedom of no-one knowing where she was. Ginette would be on the water by now, taking part in the afternoon race and probably wishing Sam could take the afternoon off, too.

She picked a stem of grass and nibbled the thick end. It tasted familiarly sweet. Immediately back in the past, she remembered a picnic with some cousins when she was six. She thought of the grassy slope and the joy of rolling down to the bottom, laughing and screaming. An only child, she vvondered now what it would have been like to have had a brother or sister and for the first time sensed Dad's sadness in not having a bigger family.

After a while Ellie stood up to retrace her steps. A few other people were exercising dogs, or doing a healthy jog, red of face and gasping.

Onward and upward, she thought as she

walked. That had been one of Dad's favourite phrases when she was a little girl. Always encouraging, he liked to point out that there was usually a good side to everything, even if you couldn't see it at the time

She smiled as at last she went down the path that led her back to her car. She felt she could deal with anything now that life, and Marsha, threw at her. A few more days and the Culmore Pavilion would be officially reopened, the art exhibition running smoothly and the music festival in full swing.

All it needed now was the news that Miss Valence would be coming home, and with care, could be present at some if not all of the festivities. With the beauty of downs, sky and sea around her, Ellie thought as she turned the key in the ignition, anything seemed possible.

By the time she got back to Bredon Court Ginette was already there replacing her sailing equipment in the cupboard allotted for her use

'Good race?' Ellie asked. 'You're back early.'

Ginette looked at her closely 'You look as if you've been at the cream, my friend. Don't tell me . . . Wonder Girl has given up and cleared off back where she came from? No such luck?'

Ellie laughed.

'I thought not.' Ginette slammed shut the cupboard door. 'Any coffee going? I want to hear the latest about Miss Valence before I visit. Sam's picking me up in about twenty minutes?'

They sat in their usual place on the low wall edging the patio. Ellie's euphoria was still with her and she found she could joke with ease about Adam and Marsha turning up at the hospital so unexpectedly. When she finished her coffee she fetched her gardening tools to do a bit of tidying up as they talked.

'You haven't put those guinea pigs of yours out in their run today,' Ginette said, taking a long swig of her coffee.

Ellie, busy with the shears, looked up from neatening the edge of the lawn.

The run was there at the far end of the garden in the shade of the sycamore tree, but it was empty as she knew. And so was the hutch when she ran across to look.

She gazed at it in alarm. 'I don't believe this!'

Ellie moved the bedding straw aside but knew she was wasting her time. The catch had been undone deliberately and then done up again. 'I fed them before I went to the hospital,' she said 'The catch was secure then. I know it was. I always check.' She felt cold suddenly.

'Then who did it?' Ginette demanded.

Ellie struggled to keep calm. 'They're here somewhere. They must be.'

'Unless they've been stolen?'

Ellie dared not think of that. Instead she began searching in the bushes and undergrowth of this shady part of the garden, oblivious of stinging nettles and brambles. She called her pets' names in a voice that shook.

Ginette found a stick and hacked at some of the weeds. Then she stopped suddenly and looked at Ellie is dismay. 'Sam,' she said 'I'd forgotten I'm supposed to be meeting him. He'll be outside waiting.'

She dashed off. The garden gate clattered open and swung back against the wall with crash. She was back at once with Sam.

He looked freshly scrubbed and vigorous in his light clothes. 'Missing pets?' he said briefly

Ellie nodded as Ginette went into hurried explanations with her face flushed with emotion.

Sam took in the situation and grabbed a stick for himself. But instead of slashing wildly at the foliage he carefully parted the brambles. 'Ouch, there're stingers here.'

'Sorry,' Ellie said 'I should have warned you

He looked round for a dock leaf but unable to see one rubbed his bare legs with a handful of grass. 'Better than nothing,' he said. 'Don't worry about it Ellie. Or about your guinea pigs. We'll find them.'

And they did, not far away after all huddled together in long grass beneath the forsythia bush close to the wall.

With a cry of delight Ellie picked them up and held their soft bodies to her face. 'Oh, my poor dears,' she murmured. Through their smooth coats she felt their hearts thumping wildly.

'Pity they can't talk,' Ginette said, breathing heavily after her exertions.

They emerged into the sunlight of the lawn. Immediately Sam went to the hutch and examined the catch. 'Nothing wrong with it,' he said

'We know that,' Ginette said scornfully. 'We looked.'

'You'll need to keep a padlock on it Ellie,' Sam said, ignoring her. 'I've got one somewhere about at my place. Like me to get it for you? It's not far. I can drop Ginette off at the hospital on the way.'

Ellie sat down on the wall with her guinea pigs in her lap, and stroked them. Sam to the rescue again, she thought as they left. Ginette was lucky to have met someone so kind and generous.

The late afternoon breeze gradually cooled her hot cheeks. The scented garden was a lovely place to be even if some of the beds needed weeding. It was a wonder that Marsha wasn't complaining. But Marsha's mind was on other things than weeds these days, plotting no doubt her next move against her great-aunt. And against her.

With a sudden clearness of mind Ellie knew why Marsha had tampered with the wording of the invitation . . . to diminish her in everyone's eyes. Especially Adam's. In her employer's, too, of course.

*   *   *

With the padlock safely in place, locked and with the key on a chair round here neck, Ellie felt happy enough about Flora and Dinah's safety to leave the garden. She and Sam had lingered for a while, chatting about sailing and the forthcoming celebrations. To his surprise he was going to be involved in a small way because he had been asked to make sure he was present at the prize-giving immediately after the opening ceremony. He had won the trophy sponsored by the Culmore.

'That's really good,' Ellie said, pleased.

'It's a deadly secret,' he said, looking furtively round as if he expected a squad of trophy police to spring out of the bushes and handcuff him.

Ellie laughed. 'Then I'm honoured to know about it in advance.'

'You and Ginette both.'

'And you expect Ginette to keep a secret?' she asked in mock amazement.

He laughed, too. 'Not really. Who knows?'

Ellie glanced up at the window of Marsha's apartment and saw a shadowy figure keeping well back. Immediately it vanished.

'What's wrong?' he said

'Ginette would have a ball with that . . . seeing Marsha watching us without wanting to be seen.'

'And you wouldn't?'

She hesitated, feeling awkward. 'I'm not sure yet of the implications,' she said 'I need to think about it.'

She was glad he didn't press it. She needed time to work out possible reasons for such an incredible act on two harmless guinea pigs. *Her* guinea pigs. Yes, that was it without a doubt. Marsha again!

Deep in thought, she said goodbye to Sam and went indoors to change out of her jeans and T-shirt into a flowered skirt and top ready for another visit to hospital.

This time she had Miss Valence to herself because Ginette had already left. Her employer was seated in a high-backed chair at the side of her bed.

'The doctor was pleased with me this afternoon,' she said as soon as she had greeted Ellie. 'I expect to come home soon, but the annoying man wouldn't tell me for certain.' Miss Valence sighed. 'I know I must be patient.'

She looked so forlorn now that Ellie leaned forward and pressed her hand. 'I'll see they understand about the Culmore,' she said.

Miss Valence brightened at the mention of the place that meant so much to her. She took such a lively interest in all that Ellie had to tell her about listening in to some of the musical rehearsals that had been taking place, that

142

Ellie returned to Bredon Court with a happy heart.

Now that most of the arrangements for the art exhibition were in place Ellie thought that time might hang heavily on her hands, but not a bit of it. Hospital visiting took care of an hour or two a day, even though others arranged to go, too. Barbara Whitlock and her sister called in most days and David was there on Wednesday evening before sailing, carrying his aunt's photo album to leave there for Miss Valence to ponder over at her leisure and promising to return for it next day because he had taken a week's holiday to be here for the start of the celebrations.

Ellie left the side ward as soon as they arrived, pleased that her employer was happily engaged. She was even more pleased to meet the staff nurse who looked after her.

The doctor's here if you'd like a word?' she said.

Would she not! Ellie hastened to the office indicated, full of questions and an urge to demand Miss Valence's release immediately.

He was an older man than she expected, slightly stooped and grey-haired. His eyes looked tired and there was a droop to the sides of his mouth.

Ellie hesitated in the doorway

'Ah, yes,' he said. His sudden smile lit up his face and she could see that he was a younger man than she had first thought. 'And you are?'

'Ellie Langley, Miss Valence's personal assistant.'

'Come in, come in. I've been hearing a lot about you, Miss Langley. You're so much more than a mere assistant, I understand. A personal friend, too, who has her welfare at heart.'

Ellie felt a warm flush on her cheeks. She smiled, knowing from his tone of voice that the news was good and she had no need to do anything but listen to what this kind man had to tell her.

Afterwards she stepped out briskly along the seafront, Daisy prancing at her side and glad of the extra walk. The good news invigorated her and she smelled the tangy air with appreciation as she quickened her pace.

She had already made sure that Miss Valence's apartment was ready and waiting for her return from hospital in the morning. She had planned lunch and shopped for it. The yellow roses and sweet honeysuckle she had arranged in a favourite vase to greet her was on the bureau and there was nothing else to do for the moment. So, a walk it would be.

The sailing dinghies were out on the water, heeling slightly to make the most of the slight breeze. She watched them round the beach mark and head out to sea again. By the time she and Daisy reached the end of the promenade and climbed down the steps to walk back along the beach the starting gun had fired for the first three boats over the line. She hoped that Ginette would be among them, and Sam, too.

Daisy skittered about among the pebbles at the water's edge, seeming not to notice that the tide was in and the hard sand she loved to explore was hidden beneath the waves. Ellie watched her for some time and then let out a loud whistle to bring her back.

Daisy came at once and Ellie attached the lead. Tail wagging and tongue hanging out, the dog came willingly up the steps at her side.

The boats were back now and she paused as they reached the sailing club to watch the activity in the boatyard. She could see Ginette cramming her sail into the sail bag as if she hated the sight of it and never wanted to see it again. Ellie looked in dismay at the fierce expression on her face as her friend spun round and saw her

'Ginette, what's happened?'

'What's happened? I'll tell you what's happened. Or not happened.' Ginette gave such an angry slap to the hull it moved out of position. Ignoring it, she picked up her belongings. Her feet squelched in her sodden sailing shoes as she came to join Ellie but she seemed not to notice the discomfort.

'Something's wrong?' Elle said, alarmed.

'Wrong?' her friend snapped. She stumped along beside her, hoisting her bag up on one shoulder.

'Calm down, Ginette, and tell me.'

'Where's Sam?' Ginette demanded. 'That's what I want to know'

'He didn't turn up to sail?'

'You can say that again. So where was he?'

Ellie wished she could tell her. She tried to think of a reason that might satisfy her friend but realised that nothing would in her present mood.

In heavy silence they walked back to Bredon Court for Ginette to leave some of her belongings in her cupboard near the kitchenette.

'We'd better go up to my place,' Ellie said before Ginette could go stamping off. 'First I must take Daisy back or Mrs Drew will think I've lost her.

Ginette remained silent as they entered the lift, her lips pursed and her hands clenched at her side. She reminded Ellie of a volcano about to burst and she was relieved to get her inside her apartment before that happened.

She hastened to make coffee and heaped two teaspoons of sugar into Ginette's mug instead of the usual one There was an emergency here even if she didn't understand what it was. So, Sam hadn't turned up to sail? There could be a hundred reasons for that but it was no good saying so. For all she knew Ginette might have some deep dread that made her fear the worst where Sam was concerned.

146

Ellie placed the mug of coffee on the table in front of her friend and took her own to drink near the window. From here she could look down on the hutch at the end of the garden and check that all was in order there. She had to squint to see it because it was almost hidden by the bushes.

'What are you looking at?' Ginette asked suspiciously. She came to join her, carrying her mug of coffee.

'Thanks to Sam the hutch is secure,' Ellie said.

But Ginette wasn't interested in any of that. 'I knew it,' she spluttered.

'Knew what?'

Ginette slammed her mug down on the window-sill, coffee flying everywhere.

Down below, seated on the patio in a reclining chair was Marsha. To her dismay Ellie could see the top of her fair head close to another one They looked as if they had been settled there for some time.

'Sam!' Ginette cried through gritted teeth.

A Growing Resentment

'There's nothing we can do about it,' Ellie said quickly. 'Just calm down.'

'Just watch me.'

Ginette looked so fierce that Ellie grabbed hold of her arm. 'Think, Ginette, think.'

'I can't think,' Ginette said, her voice trembling as she pulled free. 'Sam loves sailing. He wouldn't miss it for anything. And yet he's down there with *her*. What does it mean? What *can* it mean?' She gazed at Ellie in despair. 'I'm going down.'

'No, no, Ginette, have some sense.' Ellie felt totally inadequate to deal with this.

'She's got him hooked.' Ginette gasped. 'It's what she does.'

But suppose Sam had made the running, flattered by Marsha's interest? Ellie thought. What then?

Ginette rushed to a chair by the table, crashed down on it and sat with her head in her hands. Her shoulders shook.

Ginette was crying now with heaving sobs. Ellie pushed a box of tissues towards her and Ginette groped for one with a shaking hand.

'We were close, Sam and me,' she gasped at last, sitting up and scrubbing her face. 'Really close. What am I going to do?'

'Nothing,' Ellie said as firmly as she could.

148

'Nothing at all. Wait to hear Sam's side of things. It might be nothing more than mere friendship, a helping hand for something or other. How do you know it isn't?'

'I do know,' Ginette said fiercely. 'To give up sailing in this evening's race for her for whatever reason? I simply can't believe it.'

'Then don't.'

'You're hard, Ellie. Do you know that?'

'Just sensible,' Ellie said. She got up to clear up the mess of coffee stains on the window-sill and floor. 'We'll wait a few minutes more,' she said when she had finished. 'And then if they're still there I'll go down to the office with a pile of papers in my hand and act as if nothing's happened. Which it hasn't . . .'

Ginette gave a bleak laugh that turned into a hiccup. 'If you say so.'

Ellie wasn't at all sure that this was the right thing to do but at the moment couldn't think of anything better.

*　　　*　　　*

Over in his office at the Culmore, Adam put down the phone and leaned back in his chair. Marsha wasn't at home, or not answering. He tried her mobile and heard the ringing tone. Then it was switched off. Strange.

He made up his mind suddenly, sprang up and left the office. As he went out of the building he called a greeting to one of the musicians staggering up the steps with his cello. Now that the concerts were so close several of them had arrived early to get themselves acclimatised and he never knew when he would stumble upon someone taking advantage of an empty room for a last-minute rehearsal.

He smiled a greeting and ran nimbly down the steps, deep in thought. In spite of taking an extremely laid-back attitude to the whole affair Marsha was still officially the art exhibition organiser and he needed her input with this latest problem of deciding who should be asked to open the art exhibition and say a few suitable words now that their first choice had pulled out. It was more than likely her help would be minimal, but she must be consulted for courtesy's sake.

He glanced at his watch as he crossed the road to Bredon Court. Nine o'clock. Marsha might be anywhere but he had to check. For all he knew she might have had some accident . . . and turned off her mobile? So, no, not that. It hardly made sense.

Frowning, he rang the bell of her apartment as Ellie came down the stairs. He heard the slight sound and spun round. She looked distraught on seeing him.

'Ellie, is there anything wrong?'

'Yes, I mean no. I . . .'

'Miss Valence? There's bad news.'

'Oh, no, not that.'

'Marsha?' he said. 'Is she in, do you know? Have you come to see her?'

She shook her head. 'No, I mean yes. I think Marsha's in. Sam is with her. We saw them in the garden.'

'Ah.' Now he understood. Marsha was playing games again and upsetting Ellie in the process. He felt a surge of anger and pressed the bell harder this time'

'Come in!'

Her voice sounded welcoming but he hesitated, wanting to stand aside politely for Ellie to enter first, but afraid at the same time of witnessing her pain at seeing Marsha and Sam together.

The door opened and Sam was there. He smiled, the picture of innocence.

Adam frowned. 'I'd like to speak to Marsha.' His voice sounded sharper than he intended but the other man appeared unaware of anything amiss.

'Come in, both of you,' he said and stood aside for them to pass him.

Marsha was seated now in her chair in the sitting-room with her injured foot on the footstool. Her silky maroon skirt was spread out around her as if she had been posing for a photograph. So she wasn't in the garden as Ellie had said. Or if she had been she was a fast mover, with or without crutches.

She smiled up at Adam in a haze of perfume. 'Sam's pouring drinks,' she said. 'I

151

shan't take any excuses this time, Adam.'

He smiled in acceptance and then looked round at Ellie who had said nothing and might well be invisible for all the notice Marsha was taking of her.

'Please, not for me,' Ellie murmured as Sam asked silently with an uplifted eyebrow if she would like one, too. 'I can't stay . . . I need to put these papers in the office, that's all.' She moved towards the door.

'Very wise,' Marsha said, watching her go with complacency. She smiled at Adam. 'We've just been discussing the dance at the Culmore after the prize-giving and Sam wants to escort me there. Sweet of him, don't you think?'

Adam looked him, trying to calculate just how this had come about.

A hunted expression flicked across the other man's face. He was too much of a gentleman to argue, Adam thought with sudden sympathy. He put his glass down on the small table at his side.

'I can't allow that,' he said smoothly. 'That's my prerogative, Marsha.'

She looked delighted. 'It is?'

'I must pull rank here. I insist you withdraw the invitation, Sam.'

Marsha looked from one to the other, a small smile at the corners of her mouth. 'So one of you is going to be disappointed?'

Adam bowed his head gallantly. He was

152

glad to see that Sam was disguising his apparent disappointment with remarkable ease.

'I must be on my way now, Marsha,' Sam said quickly. 'It seems that there's something pressing to be discussed between the two of you. Thank you for your hospitality.'

No fool, then, Adam thought.

For a moment Marsha looked disconcerted but as Adam sat down and picked up his glass she smiled at Sam. 'You'll come and see me again?'

Sam muttered something and left so hurriedly the door was slightly open. As Adam got up to close it he was just in time to see Ellie waiting outside.

He returned to Marsha and the job in hand with a heavy heart.

Ellie put the papers into the study and tidied the pile already there on the desk to give her some moments to think about what had just happened. Coming down here had served no useful purpose. How could it? All she had done was to prove to Adam how ineffectual she was around Marsha. She locked the door and replaced the key and for a moment hesitated outside Marsha's door.

'Ellie!' Sam said in surprise. 'Still here?'

He looked decidedly flustered and his fair hair was sticking up in peaks where he had obviously run his hand through it.

She smiled, pleased to see he had escaped,

too. 'I'm only here because I'm dreading going back upstairs to Ginette.'

'Ginette!'

The girl you promised to meet at the sailing club for the afternoon race. She's none too happy"

'Because I failed to show up,' he said bitterly .That one in there's a tiger but I've no excuse. Let's go for a drink. I need it.'

'And let Ginette think she has two rivals?'

He groaned. 'I've been a fool.'

'I know how it was, Sam, believe me.'

'I don't know how it happened. She's quite a girl and somehow there I was seated in her garden with a glass of poison in my hand lending a sympathetic ear.'

'Poison?'

'So it seemed. Wine to anyone else.'

Ellie smiled. 'So all is well really. I just need to convince Ginette.'

'Ginette's up there in your place?' he said eagerly.

'Don't even think of it,' she said 'Imagine the almighty row if you came up at the moment. Ginette would come storming down to attack Marsha personally and the whole building would be agog. I'll tell her you want to see her at once now you've escaped. It's the best I can do.'

'The late night café round the corner?'

'It'll give her time to calm down.'

'I see what you mean.'

'I'll put in a good word for you, Sam.'

'She's full of character, Ginette,' he said admiringly 'Thanks, Ellie. You're a good pal. I owe you one.'

'You've done plenty for me already, Sam.'

'But not as important as this,' he said 'I shan't forget.

*   *   *

Thursday was a busy day, as Ellie had known it would be. The screens were due to be delivered at eight-thirty and Ellie made sure she was there even though it was Marsha's responsibility. No-one could tell her what time Miss Valence could be expected home, but she was advised to telephone the hospital at eleven o'clock.

To her surprise she saw Marsha as soon as she went into the exhibition room. She was seated near the door, nodding and smiling as each helper greeted her. She frowned as she saw Ellie. 'I thought you'd have better things to do,' she said, her voice like ice.

'I'm here to give what help I can.'

'Then get on with something. And keep away from Adam.'

Ellie made no reply but moved on and kept well back among all the activity so that she could examine her checklist and keep an eye on all that was going on

Adam was there, too, dressed in jeans and

155

T-shirt, helping lift the heavy screens into place. He acknowledged Ellie with a brief nod. Once or twice he paused to check with Marsha where each screen should go and Ellie could see by the hand gestures that Marsha was leaving it all to him, but doing so in a way that was likely to appeal to his superior expertise.

After a while, seeing how absorbed he was, Marsha struggled to her feet and reached for her crutches. This was Ellie's chance to have a word with her in private. She had to make sure that Marsha was aware that Miss Valence was coming home today.

'I'm to ring the hospital soon,' she told her 'They'll tell me what time your great-aunt can be expected home.'

The flash of impatience in Marsha's expression was gone so quickly Ellie hoped she had imagined it.

'What of it?' Marsha said, preparing to leave. 'She won't be able to come to the celebrations tomorrow surely? The festival organiser wanted her to open the show since I can hardly do that myself as I've arranged it all.' She gave a scornful laugh. 'I soon put a stop to that idea.'

Ellie said nothing but she glanced at Adam, still working hard. He looked exhausted as he heaved another screen into position and held it steady while two of the helpers made sure it was secure.

The handing-in time for the artists to bring

156

their paintings wasn't for another hour. Someone had arranged some long tables near the door for the paintings to be unwrapped and checked. Everything seemed in order.

'Coffee, anyone?' she called.

There was a clamour of acceptance. She made Adam's and carried it across to him. He took it from her gratefully.

'I need your advice, Ellie,' he said 'You heard that the original choice to open the proceedings can't do it? Any ideas?'

She frowned. 'Miss Valence might be able to suggest someone. She'll be home soon and I'll ask her. I need to go across and phone the hospital soon.'

'Do it from my office.'

She smiled. 'It'll be good to have her home again.'

He nodded without comment, obviously deep in thought. The lines at the side of his mouth seemed deeper than usual and there was a decided droop to his shoulders. The responsibility seemed to have drained a great deal of energy from him and she was sorry. He would be relieved when it was all over.

'You'll let me know if she comes up with someone good?' he said.

'I will,' she promised.

And that was all. She left the Culmore feeling disappointed that they hadn't had more to say to each other.

Bredon Court seemed like home again now

the Miss Valence was back and looking almost her old self.

With a light heart Ellie settled her in her chair by the window. She was able to tell her that everything over at the Culmore was going well.

'Apart from needing someone to preside at the opening ceremony,' she said.

Miss Valence smiled. 'I wanted Barbara Whitlock to do it from the first but was overruled. Now I might get my way.'

'Barbara Whitlock?'

'Her great-uncle was one of the first trustees when the Culmore Pavilion opened just before the war. Marjorie Lindle's, too, of course, as they're sisters.'

Ellie looked at her in surprise. 'I didn't know their great-uncle was involved with the Culmore.'

'No reason why you should, my dear. That's why they're living here. I felt a special tie to them, you see, after what happened, and when Marjorie was widowed it seemed a good idea. Her son was at university then, of course. A few years ago now.'

'David. And now he's coming back here to live.'

'He told you that?

'He seems happy about it.'

'Apparently he's got his eye on a flat for himself along the seafront. So suitable.' Miss Valence had the same secret smile on her lips that reminded Ellie of Marsha. Her quick suggestion for Miss Whitlock to open the proceedings was suitable, too.

Barbara Whitlock . . . the name seemed familiar in another context, Ellie thought, but she couldn't think how. Never mind. Adam would be pleased to hear about the suggestion.

She phoned him from the phone here in her employer's apartment.

'Excellent,' he said 'I'll call on Miss Whitlock this afternoon. Would it be in order to call on Miss Valence to thank her?'

'She'll be pleased to see you,' Ellie said.

She smiled as she put the phone down. Everything was going well. She would spend the rest of the morning over in the exhibition room in case anything cropped up that needed her attention, and then after lunch she would be free to walk Daisy before visiting the Culmore again to check the progress being made with hanging the exhibits.

*   *   *

The exhibition room was transformed. Ellie looked round in surprise and pleasure at the array of paintings hanging on the screens and all round the walls. Someone knew what they were doing to make the exhibition look so professional.

The last of the helpers was packing up now and promising that there would be a team here

159

early tomorrow to do all the last-minute things like checking the information details beside each exhibit.

Ellie thanked her, marvelling that Marsha wasn't interested enough to appreciate the excellent job that had been done by the band of volunteers.

Slowly she circumnavigated the room, pausing at each painting to examine it first from a distance and then close up. Such variety in subjects and genres, she thought. And so much talent. Cheselton-on-Sea should be proud.

She particularly liked an oil painting of Beachy Head at sunset, admiring the effect of the thick paint and bold strokes that only brought the work to life from a distance. Close up it seemed like a muddle of fiery colours. She moved back slowly to see at exactly which point it made sense to the eye.

'Applied with a palette knife, of course.'

She swung round to see Adam, changed now into a blue shirt and fresh jeans and with hair still damp from a shower.

'I'm sorry to startle you,' he said 'You were totally absorbed.'

'I love it.'

'It's got a high price on it.'

'And no wonder,' she said.

He smiled. 'So you're having a private preview of the exhibition?'

'Just checking to see the progress made with

setting things up.'

'And you're impressed?'

'Aren't you?'

'It takes a lot to impress me, but . . yes, I am. The team has worked wonders with little supervision and I'm proud of them. I think we'll have to make the exhibition an annual event in future.'

She glowed with pleasure although she had only played a small part in the preparation. Maybe next year she could be more involved.

His face clouded. 'If I'm lucky enough to be made permanent here, of course.'

'Is that in doubt?'

'I hope not.'

She had finished looking at the painting now and knew she must get back to Bredon Court because Miss Valence might need her. She made a move towards the door.

'I admire Miss Valence very much,' he said as he accompanied her. 'She's a fine lady. It's fortunate for us that she has so much spirit. I'm delighted she feels well enough to be at the opening ceremony tomorrow and at the prize-giving, too, to watch her great-niece present the Culrnore Trophy. A proud moment for her.'

Ellie smiled and agreed as they went out into the entrance hail and she waited for him to lock the door behind them. 'She's going to give the party afterwards a miss, though,' she said. 'And so is Mrs Drew and her cousin.

161

They're planning to spend the evening with her. It means I can enjoy myself over here with a clear conscience.'

Well of course you'll want to be here for the dance, too, as well as for the prize-giving?'

Ginette was the one who needed to be here for that, Ellie thought. She hadn't seen her since early yesterday evening and hoped this meant that she was engrossed with Sam again and he with her.

Adam paused as they reached his office. 'I'll be here for a few hours more yet, so I'll say goodnight,' he said. He made a gesture of dismissal.

It seemed like a brush-off but there was no reason why it should. She had things to do, too.

A Threat Of Blackmail

Ellie fastened the latch on her guinea pigs' hutch, slid the key into the padlock and locked it.

'You're safe now, my beauties,' she told them. 'Sleep tight.'

As she turned away she saw a movement at Marsha's window and knew she was being watched. When she went inside it was no surprise to find Marsha waiting for her at the bottom of the stairs.

'So you're taking more care of those precious pets of yours now, are you?' Marsha greeted her in a scornful voice.

Ellie felt her colour rise. 'It's become necessary to lock their hutch, yes.'

'And what exactly do you mean by that?'

'I think you know full well.'

Marsha's eyes glittered. 'Are you accusing me of something?'

'Now why should I do that?'

One word of suspicion out of you and I'll see that Adam Merville is finished in Cheselton-on-Sea. Isn't it enough that you've wormed your way into my great-aunt's good books expecting she'll change her will in your favour without making a play for him as well?'

'That's outrageous on both counts.'

Marsha looked exultant. 'Outrageous or not that's the deal. If you don't get your bags packed at once and leave tomorrow see that Adam leaves here under a cloud.'

Ellie was appalled. 'You can't do that!'

'Can't I just? You just wait and see, Miss Butter-Wouldn't-Melt-In-Her-mouth. I'll stand there in front of all the dignitaries and everyone who matters landing accusations on his devious head that'll keep the newspapers going for weeks. The press photographers will have a field day.'

Ellie felt as if the floor was rising to hit her She clutched the banisters to steady herself.

But Marsha hadn't finished. 'And what's

more,' she added triumphantly. 'I'll refuse to have anything to do with the festivities. I'll refuse to attend the opening ceremony and prize-giving as well. And just see how that affects my great-aunt!'

Ellie bowed her head and tried to compose herself enough to answer her but by the time she recovered Marsha had gone.

She took deep painful breaths as she climbed the stairs to the first floor. Were these merely empty threats or had Marsha the power to do as she promised? Marsha's confidence was chilling.

Outside her employer's apartment Ellie paused, knowing she couldn't go in just yet and act as if nothing had happened. At that moment the door of the apartment opposite opened and David Lindle appeared carrying his bulky hold-all.

'Ellie? Is that you?' He hesitated on seeing her leaning against the wall. 'You look as if you've had a bit of a shock.'

'Who is it?' came his aunt's strong voice from inside the apartment. She came to the door, took a look at Ellie and ushered her inside. Then with a nod she signalled to her nephew to come in, too, and shut the door behind him.

'Get the kettle on, Marjorie,' she said

Ellie was glad to sink down in the chair David pulled out and be fussed over by his mother for the next few minutes.

164

Barbara Whitlock eyed Ellie closely. 'I can see you've had words,' she pronounced. 'And I don't need to ask who with. Take no notice. She's worthless, that one. Truth will out. It's my guess she finally snapped when she couldn't oust you from Miss Valence's affections and when someone you care about started paying you the attention, she wanted it for herself. We're not all the fools as she likes to think us even if we *are* old crocks.'

'What are you talking about?' her sister asked.

David looked from one to the other. 'I can't begin to understand what's going on, either,' he said

Miss Whitlock's eyes narrowed. 'Ellie and I understand each other and I see you do, too, my lad, after she's gone. This is the last chance for that wicked one to get at you, Ellie, and she's desperate. But you're strong. Remember that. You can cope with anything and come out on top. Courage, my dear, courage!'

Courage was definitely what she wanted now, Ellie thought, but where was it when she needed it?

Fortified by the sugary tea David's mother made her drink she got to her feet. 'I must go,' she said, 'Thank you for your kindness.'

'Kindness, pah!' Miss Whitlock exclaimed. 'Support is what you need and I shall see you get it.'

David held the door open further and

stood well back to let her through. Heartened, Ellie crossed the landing to her employer's apartment. She heard the music as she went inside. A full orchestra was playing one of the Straus waltzes and on the TV screen in the sitting-room was a colourful ballroom of swirling glamour.

Miss Valence smiled at her. 'You're looking pale and tired and no wonder, Ellie. Come and sit down and rest. Such a lovely programme I'm watching. It won't be quite like that tomorrow evening, I know, my dear, but I hope you'll enjoy it all the same.'

Ellie nodded. 'It'll be a wonderful occasion.'

'A well-deserved reward for all your hard work and kindness to me. I've had some visitors this afternoon as you know and now you're here, Ellie. I have to tell you there was a phone call for you just half an hour ago. I told your father you would phone him as soon as you could.'

'Dad?'

'Do it now. Ellie my dear. And give him my regards.' She clicked on the mute button on the remote control. Ellie picked up the receiver. 'Dad?'

His voice sounded as if it was in the same room. 'Just to wish you a happy day tomorrow, Ellie, love,' he said, a smile in his voice. 'A big day for you all. Amanda's been out shopping and got herself kitted out. She looks amazing. There's a chance we might be with

166

you after all.'

'Oh, Dad, that's wonderful!'

'We might only show up at the last minute if that's all right with you.'

'I'll leave tickets for you at the door,' she promised. 'And I'll warn the person who's there to look out for you.'

'Right you are then, love. See you!'

A short call but for quality she couldn't beat it. She smiled as she sat down beside Miss Valence and asked her what food she would like her to prepare for an early supper.

*　　　*　　　*

Ellie woke three times in the night, Marsha's vindictive words hammering in her head and preventing her from getting back to sleep the third time. For a while she lay and listened to a lone bird greeting the dawn and thought of Ginette's likely reaction to the latest development with Marsha. But of course she dare not tell her.

One thing was certain. She must pack her bags immediately. She leapt out of bed, pulled on her thick dressing gown and set to work.

By the time sunshine was stealing into the garden down below and highlighting the white clematis on the wall she had almost finished. The kitchen equipment could be dealt with later but first she needed a coffee, good and strong.

She carried it across to the window and gazed down on the garden. From here, of course, it looked foreshortened. From Marsha's apartment on the ground floor there had been an excellent view of her guinea pigs' hutch and of everything else, too. It was clear that Marsha has been watching her moves at every opportunity. And planning something like this all along?

Ellie had a sudden picture in her mind of her return from Dad and Amanda's wedding when she had danced on the lawn with Flora and Dinah. The grass had been soft beneath her bare feet and the scent of honeysuckle filled the air and from her employer's open window had floated the violin music she loved to revel in now she could no longer make music for herself.

And Adam had come. She could see him now as she had seen him then, tall and good looking, full of a special charm that seemed to speak to herself alone. She had known from that moment that he was someone special, although she had pretended otherwise. How carefree she had been then! But now Marsha's threats hung over her like a dark cloud.

Miss Valence's courage in working hard for the preservation of the Culmore Pavilion even though at times she was full of pain was phenomenal. There would be concerts throughout the summer months now and she would enjoy every one. They would bring back happy memories of her youth when the musical world was her life. And there was the added thrill that her great-grandfather was instrumental in the opening of the Culmore all those years ago. Because of the family connection the Culmore Pavilion was her great love and the re-opening of it would be a highlight of her life. For her great-niece to refuse to attend the celebrations would hurt her to the quick. She didn't deserve that.

And Adam. She had no doubt that Marsha was capable of carrying out her threat here, too. Adam had done a good job here, but the machinations of a vindictive girl had power to ruin him. She couldn't let that happen.

She stood at the window for a long time while her coffee, unnoticed, became stone-cold.

*   *   *

'Barbara Whitlock phoned,' her employer told her when Ellie took in her early morning tea. 'Some tale or other about you going over there at once to run your eye over her speech for the opening.'

'At this time of the morning?'

'The sooner the better, she said.'

Miss Whitlock in her khaki-coloured dressing gown looked so much like a ferocious bear that Ellie smiled.

'Nothing to smile at, young woman. We've

serious business here.'

Ellie was immediately contrite 'Your speech?'

'Speech be damned. Serious I said.'

Ellie bit her lip.

'I've been doing a bit of research since you were here when that nephew of mine let out that he thought he saw someone very much like Marsha walking briskly ahead of him on platform ten at Waterloo. David's a bit loopy at times, I know, but still. I've hit on a plan if you agree. That cleaning girl's got a head on her shoulders.'

'Ginette? But where . . .'

'At the sailing club do last night.

'You were there?'

'And why not? I've a relation who's a member after all. David took me along after a bit of pressure.'

Ellie felt bewildered. She tried to imagine Miss Whitlock striding in to the bar in her sensible shoes looking like an avenging angel.

'But you didn't tell Ginette . . .?'

'Conjecture only, remember. Least known soonest mended. This Culmore business is important to Lola Valence for two reasons. Ginette pointed out at once that shock would most likely kill your employer if you weren't there to look after her. Exaggerated perhaps, but I got the gist. Lola loves and trusts you, Ellie. We can't go ahead unless you agree. As I said I've got a plan between the three of us.

170

Sam's his name. And David. He's a soft fool but he knows what he's got to do.'

'There's something I can't tell anyone,' Ellie said. 'I may decide to leave. I may *have* to leave.'

Miss Whitlock gave her a stern look. 'Well, it's your decision. No-one can make it for you. Trust, Ellie, trust.'

Ellie stared at her. Trust was the most difficult thing to do with so much at stake. She needed to think long and hard about this

'I'll get back to you,' she said.

'There's not long to think about it. I need to know your decision at once. Time's pressing.'

Ellie knew that only too well. She returned to Miss Valence with much on her mind.

Miss Whitlock had said that it was important to her for two reasons, she thought as she laid her employer's breakfast tray. Her grandfather, of course, but who else? The man who meant a lot to her and who had never returned from the Second World War? Edgar Whitlock whom Adam so closely resembled?

Whitlock . . a co-incidence?

Miss Valence had left her scrapbook on her table and seconds later Ellie found the photo of the dark-haired young man who had meant so much to her employer. Deep in the recesses of her memory something stirred. Miss Whitlock's great-uncle had also been a founder trustee of the Culmore. So if her assumption was correct and Edgar Whitlock,

171

a violinist, was a relation of his, certain things clicked into place. Miss Valence's total interest in the future of the Cumnore was even more understandable now. Anyone normal would surely have been proud? But not Marsha. Because of her, Ellie Langley, Marsha was willing to endanger all this if she didn't obey her commands. And Adam, too, who so like Edgar, was to be part of her revenge.

It must not be allowed to happen.

This was the worst decision she had ever had to make. And the most important.

How dare Marsha seek to hurt so many people? *Adam, oh, Adam*, she thought, close to tears.

Instead of running away she would put her trust in Barbara Whitlock.

*   *   *

Ginette arrived holding her cleaning gear in front of her like a shield while Ellie was attempting to force down her toast and marmalade.

'You cleaned the apartment yesterday,' Ellie said in surprise. She dropped the half-eaten toast on her plate and pushed it to one side.

'I needed an excuse to be here, didn't I? So what's the latest?'

Ellie looked at her warily. 'About what?'

'Is it safe to talk?' Ginette glanced round

172

the room as if she expected curious spectators to be hiding behind the furniture.

'Miss Valence is resting on her bed for a little while. She won't hear us.'

Ginette discarded her cleaning materials and sat down at the table. She stared hard at Ellie. 'Now tell me all. I'm guessing you know quite a bit already.'

'Not until last night I didn't. And not enough. I've gathered there's a crisis because Miss Whitlock suddenly appeared and carried Sam and David off somewhere to make plans.'

'I didn't know till last night either and then not what Miss Whitlock would like to do,' Ellie said. 'Marsha's ultimatum to me was a complete shock. If I don't do what she says and leave Cheselton for good she'll ruin Adam and bring disrepute on the Cuirnore.'

'That's blackmail! You're not going to let her get away with it? And anyway how do you know she won't do as she threatens whether you go or not?'

Her friend sounded so indignant that Ellie felt buoyed up with her support.

'She threatens to stand up in front of everybody at the opening ceremony and do her worst,' she said 'I can't bear the thought that Miss Valence will be devastated . . .' Ellie paused, struck by a sudden thought.

'Why are you looking like that?'

'I'm not sure. I've got to think.'

'Thinking won't do any good, my friend. It's

173

drastic action that's needed.'

'Thinking time first. This is important, Ginette. Really important. I'm going out. Now.'

'Go for it. And then stop her somehow. I'll be here for the next twenty minutes and will keep an eye on Miss Valence. And Ellie, good luck"

She needed more than good luck. She needed strength and determination and the certainty that Marsha's aims were based solely on greed and selfishness and must never be allowed to flourish. Miss Valence was elderly but she was no fool. She had seen the potential in Adam as others had. Thousands of pounds had been spent on work to update the Culmore Pavilion and bring it into the twenty-first century to be an asset to the town as it had been in its earliest days.

Ellie sat on the pebbles with her back pressed hard against the wall of the promenade and gazed at the surging sea. She picked up a piece of dry seaweed and held it to her nose. It smelled of nothing but brittle rottenness. She crumbled it in her hand and dropped the pieces.

Would people really believe any lies or scandal about Adam that Marsha came out with, just supposing she had any proof? The hall would be full, the press there in force, Miss Valence seated in a place of honour. The place would be in uproar.

Ellie listened to the crash of the waves on the pebbles, deploring her indecision. She thought of how upset her employer would be if she vanished without warning. Miss Valence hadn't yet regained her strength from the shock of her collapse just days ago. This might well be enough to precipitate another more serious one. Had Marsha thought of that in her vindictive ultimatum to her? If Ellie were no longer here, disgraced in Adam's eyes for running away at a crucial time, the field would be open to her. But if Ellie ignored the ultimatum and Marsha carried out her threat the shock of the crowd's reaction would most likely finish her great-aunt.

Either way Marsha would be the winner. Or so she believed.

But how could she do that when she threatened to boycott the celebrations? There was a flaw in Marsha's vindictive outpourings.

Ellie picked up a stone and aimed it at the sea. It fell short and she tried another. This time it landed in the surf with a satisfactory splash. She stood up, suddenly knowing what she must do.

A Public Scene

Miss Valance had chosen what she was going to wear for the opening ceremony and now all Ellie had to do was to locate her accessories and make sure her black patent shoes had the brightest shine she could manage.

'And my velvet reticule,' she said 'Oh, my dear, I can't imagine when I saw that little evening bag last.'

'Would you like me to look for it?'

Her employer looked at her gratefully. 'If you would, Ellie. I feel in such a muddle I can't really think. I want to look my best. I want Marsha to be proud of me this evening and there's so little time.'

'Plenty of time,' Ellie assured her. And so there was for Miss Valence to get ready, but not to get back to Miss Whitlock waiting to hear her decision.

The phone rang.

'Barbara Whitlock here,' said an imperious voice.

'Oh, Miss Whitlock, I . . .'

'She's planning something,' Miss Valence said. 'I've known her for years. She doesn't change.'

'She wants to see me. I won't be long,' Ellie said, already on her way to the door.

Barbara Whitlock was waiting for her.

'Well?'

Ellie took a deep breath. 'I'm not leaving.I'll help all I can.'

'Well done. Your part is to escort Lola Valence to the opening ceremony and to make sure she sits on the second seat of the front row nearest the door. You must sit on the outside next to her, ready to escort her out at a moment's notice if she needs privacy. We'll be taking a risk here. I'll be on stage doing the speechmaking and talk for exactly five minutes.'

Ellie was confused. Where was all this leading?

'I'm coming to that,' Miss Whitlock said as if Ellie had spoken. 'Sam and David will be primed for action. I've good reason to believe that young Marsha is a self-seeking fraud and we're going to prove it in a public way that will make her look ridiculous. She may be Lola's great-niece but that doesn't stop her being a nasty piece of work.'

'But I don't see . . .'

'You don't have to see at the moment. It's best you don't know the details and are as surprised as the rest of them. Your body language will prove that. Then you can't be held responsible for what happens. But you need to be on duty. I need your co-operation.'

'You have that,' Ellie said

'You have to trust us, Ellie. Are you strong enough for that?'

177

Ellie was silent, thinking of the harm that Marsha was planning to do in the name of revenge.

Miss Whitlock gave a bark of a laugh. 'Marsha Valence deserves to be exposed for what she is.'

'But her great-aunt doesn't deserve to witness what you are planning.'

'That's as may be,' Miss Whitlock said with a firmness Ellie knew was rock hard. 'Lola's got a well of strength inside that frail body of hers. And see you do your bit, Ellie. Make sure that horrendous great-niece of hers knows you haven't gone away as she ordered. Our plan depends on her knowing that!'

*   *   *

Her employer's velvet evening bag was where Ellie thought it would be along with her long lacy gloves. No problem there. The problem was with Ellie herself, because she couldn't relax however hard she tried. She wished Miss Whitlock had told her exactly what would happen so that she could feel confident that the plan would work.

She phoned Ginette's home mid morning but her mother said she had no idea where she was if she wasn't at work at Bredon Court.

Daisy's walk was shorter than usual this morning because Ellie wanted to spend time with her guinea pigs, watched, hopefully, by

178

Marsha. Then she took, herself over to the Culmore in case Marsha was there.

The caterer's van was parked in the car park handy for the side door and inside the building people were bustling about. In the exhibition room everything was in order. She had a quick check that the sheets of stick-on red dots to indicate that paintings were sold were handy on the desk.

There was no sign of Marsha. Or of Adam.

She met him halfway up the steps as she was leaving the building. He wasn't expecting to see her because he looked up at her from a step or two below with obvious surprise. She could imagine why. Marsha at work again with more malicious lies. She smiled.

'Hello, Adam.'

He took the two steps in one stride. 'Ellie, I'm so glad to see you.'

'Me, too.'

She heard the warmth in his voice but kept her eyes downcast to hide her own delight in case she had misjudged his reaction. This was a big day for him. He would be keyed up to a height of emotion for something that had meant the world to him for weeks, the culmination of his dedicated work and one which could result in his success in being offered the permanent position he so much desired.

'Miss Valence is well?' he asked.

'Resting now and looking forward to this

evening.'

'And you, too, Ellie?'

She raised her eyes. 'Of course.'

'There are reserved seats for you both in prime position in the centre of the front row.'

'At one side would be better. The side near the door. If that's all right?'

'Of course. I'll see to it at once.'

She knew he understood the reason for that, or thought he did. She didn't even understand it herself but was relieved that it was sorted out without argument before they arrived this evening.

'I must get back to her,' she said, although it was hard to make the first move.

Getting ready for the evening was hard, too, because her fingers felt like sausages as she struggled to do up the tiny pearl buttons on the back of her best dress. That done at last, she picked up the delicate gold and pearl earrings that had been her father's gift to her at his wedding.

She held them for a moment in her hand, remembering her concern for him that day with a clearness that was startling. But this wasn't the moment to dwell on that.

She had allowed plenty of time for helping her employer to prepare for the opening ceremony. Miss Valence had insisted on a taxi for the short distance to the Culmore rather than Ellie driving her and asked Ellie to contact her great-niece and offer her a lift

180

as well.

Ellie lifted the receiver, her heart beat quickening. Marsha gave a short triumphant laugh. 'In a taxi . . . or an ambulance?'

Ellie, seething, made no reply.

'So you're still here then?' Marsha sounded jubilant and let a long pause develop before her next words. 'Adam has made arrangements to collect me, of course. You can tell my great-aunt that. It'll make her day.'

But Miss Valence only nodded vaguely when Ellie told her, more concerned about how lovely Ellie looked in the dress she hadn't worn since the wedding.

The buzz of expectation as they entered the Culmore Pavilion raised Ellie's spirits considerably. Miss Valence, too, looked happy as she seated herself in the seat allocated and looked round to see who else had arrived early.

The room looked beautiful and smelled delightfully of wild flower meadows. But how could that be? Ellie noticed the lighted candles in glass dishes on the desk on the platform. From there, of course. She sniffed appreciatively.

The chairs on the platform were beginning to fill with dignitaries of the town, some of whom had a word with Miss Valence as they passed her. Then Adam was there. He looked magnificent in the suit he was wearing when she had first met him and his shirt as pristine

181

white. But his face was tanned now as if he spent long hours in the sunshine instead of in his office in the Culmore working hard for this moment.

He waited in the doorway and then escorted Marsha to her seat on the platform. He took her crutches from her, helped her up the steps and made sure she was settled comfortably in the first chair at the near end of the row that bore her name card.

Ellie watched him glance at the desk and then back at Marsha. Perhaps he was dazzled, as the others obviously were, by her silvery dress that flowed round her slim body in folds of elegant grace. Her fair hair was piled high with tendrils falling across her forehead. She looked stunning.

Marsha shot a look of cunning at Ellie and then smiled at her great-aunt. Miss Valence, Ellie saw, made no acknowledgement. Instead she turned to speak to the person in the row behind.

So what did that mean? Ellie was so engrossed in working that out that she didn't at first notice Ginette. When her friend came to speak to her she looked in wonder at her long dark skirt and beaded top that made her look taller and slimmer.

'Wow, Ginette,' she said. 'You look amazing.'

'So do you, my friend,' Ginette hissed in her ear, and then vanished among the audience.

The proceedings were about to begin. The hum of conversation gradually ceased as Adam stood at the desk to welcome everyone and to introduce Miss Barbara Whitlock, whom they were fortunate enough to have with them this evening to re-open the Culmore Pavilion.

Ellie thrilled at his words. Standing there at this auspicious moment he looked so supremely confident she forgot Marsha's threats and the fear of what she might do. She felt part of it all, part of the glamour and the magic. Only when Miss Whitlock came forward and he sat down in her vacated chair did she remember with a jolt.

Ellie could see that Barbara Whitlock was enjoying this moment as she felt for her spectacles in the bag she carried over one arm.

The audience settled back to listen as she spoke movingly of the first opening in 1938 and what the Culmore Pavilion, modern for its time, had meant to the town and the work that had recently been done to return it to its former glory.

'And now,' she concluded after her allotted five minutes of riveting talk, 'I have the pleasure of declaring this magnificent building open once again. The Culmore Pavilion!'

The applause and cheering continued for several minutes.

When it subsided she waved Adam forward. 'And now I give you Mr Adam Merville, our festival organiser, whose remarkable work and insight has surely earned him the right to become the permanent manager of the Culmore.'

More applause.

Adam smiled. 'And now, everyone, we come to the presentation of the Culmore Trophy for the winner of the Culmore Sailing Race held yesterday,' he said. 'Miss Marsha Valence, beloved great-niece of Miss Lola Valence who herself is the grandaughter of one of the founder trustees, will present it to the winner, Sam Gerard.'

Ellie saw Sam standing at the side of the stage.

Miss Whitlock stepped forward again. 'May I just add something, Mr Merville,' she said her voice ringing out in the hall. 'Marsha came to Cheselton-on-Sea to organise the art exhibition for us in spite of being in great pain from a broken ankle. She battled bravely on, moving herself about on crutches which my nephew, David, is holding ready for her as you see. A round of applause, please, for a very courageous young lady!' She turned smilingly to Marsha.

Miss Valence sat impassively as if turned to stone as for the third time the applause faded.

'Now, my dear, is your golden moment,' Miss Whitlock said. 'I believe you have something important to say to us?'

Bravely wiping her eyes with a lacy handkerchief Marsha got unsteadily to her feet and held out her hand for one of her crutches. But David, misunderstanding, moved away out of reach. The suddenly realising what he should have done he stumbled over his feet, got them entangled with the crutch and fell heavily to the floor.

The audience loved it. David got to his feet and looked behind him. With his back to everyone the tear in the seat of his trousers was plainly seen. Even Miss Valence joined in the laughter that followed.

Overcome with confusion David moved to the side of the platform taking the crutches with him.

'What a fool,' someone behind Ellie muttered.

But Ellie wasn't so sure. She had seen the slight nod of conspiracy between Sam and David.

Sam moved forward towards Marsha and whispered something in her ear. The effect was electric. With a cry of rage Marsha rushed towards her crutches, but finding David moving off the platform with them she jumped off, too. There was a second's surprised silence before laughter broke out.

Marsha gave an anguished look round then bolted for the door colliding with two latecomers. One of them let out a cry as she was knocked to the floor. 'My baby, oh my baby!'

'Amanda!' At once Ellie was with her

uttering words of comfort.

'I'm all right,' Amanda cried, tears streaming down her face as John Langley took over and with Ellie's aid helped his young wife outside where a chair was instantly found.

'Did she hurt you?' Ellie demanded, filled with such rage she could hardly breathe. 'Where is she? I'll kill her for this!'

John Langley was already phoning for an ambulance. 'Ellie, my love, go back in,' he said 'This is just to ake sure that all's well. That's all. She'll be all right.'

'You're sure?' Ellie said, tears streaming.

'We'll talk later.'

She left them then and slipped back inside as the talk and laughter subsided. Before Adam spoke his eyes sought Ellie's. She saw his expression of anxiety and gave him a nod of assurance.

'I think it will be best if we wait until later to present the trophy,' he said. 'But now, ladies and gentlemen, you will find wine and canapes waiting in the exhibition room. The art exhibition is now open.'

A Loving Calm

'I should like to take a look at the exhibition before I leave,' Miss Valence said.

She didn't seem a bit put out, Ellie thought.

186

Could it be that she had come to realise exactly how the great-niece she had idolised had behaved? If so she was an even more remarkable lady than Ellie had thought.

Miss Valence said nothing about Marsha as Ellie escorted her round and she looked carefully at each exhibit. When Adam joined them she greeted him calmly. Her back held straight, she walked ahead of them as if unaware of the traumatic events that had just taken place.

'What a wonderful lady,' Adam said quietly to Ellie. 'I admire her more than I can say. I shall personally see that she has the best seat in the house for the concerts she wishes to attend.'

'All of them, I expect.'

He laughed. 'And you, Ellie, have had to put up with Marsha and her tricks. It can't have been easy.'

She smiled.

The red dot placed near the painting of Beachy Head took her by surprise. 'I don't wonder it's been sold already,' she murmured.

'Disappointed?' Adam asked.

'Someone will have pleasure in it,' she said. But she took a backward glance as they moved on, thinking that there were more important things in life than envying the purchaser of a painting. Dad and Amanda's baby for one. Her brother or sister! Although desperately worried, she was relieved beyond measure that she could be glad for them and glad for herself, too. She had no doubt now of Dad's happiness with his young wife.

She was reminded suddenly of the lovely cream photo album she had been going to buy Amanda for her birthday. It might still be there. She would look first thing tomorrow, she thought. She smiled as she imagined it full of baby pictures.

*   *   *

'He's a pleasant young man,' Miss Valence said as Ellie helped her into her apartment. 'He deserves the best and that best was not my great-niece. I realise I was a foolish old woman to think so now that I've seen at last how Marsha really is. We'll talk of it no more Adam Merville deserves the position he'll be offered at the Culmore and he'll get it with my blessing.'

Ellie felt warm colour flood her face but could say nothing. She knew that Marsha had gone from Bredon Court because Ginette, dashing into the exhibition room with Sam just as they were leaving, indicated as much with an expressive shrug of her shoulders.

She would fill in the details later when Ellie returned to the Culmore for the evening celebrations. Marsha gone, Adam in the position he coveted . . . and yet she still felt a

188

slight emptiness deep down.

She smiled. 'I'm pleased to hear that Miss Valence.' Her employer patted her arm. 'And now you must get back to him,' she said.

'You're a good girl, and my heart if full because it will seem that I haven't lost you Thank you Eloise, my dear.'

Ellie closed the garden door behind her and walked across the grass in the scented dusk thinking of Adam. And there he was waiting for her. Surprise mingled with joy in a wave of longing that seemed right for just such a moment.

She couldn't quite read his expression in the half-light but what she thought she saw added to her confusion.

'You've come,' she said.

'I knew you'd be here. I wanted to thank you in private for the way Marsha was stopped from her revenge on me and on the music festival.'

'But I did nothing!'

'You have good friends who love and support you and were prepared to take an enormous risk. I know how it was with David, and his aunt and your fiancé and . . .'

'Fiancé?' Ellie said in surprise. 'I have no fiancé.'

The second's deep silence was full of significance.

She felt her eyes shine. 'I think we've had this conversation before but the other way round. I haven't got a fiancé, either. Sad, isn't it?'

'Not for me,' Adam said firmly. Then he laughed. 'I was beginning to suspect the truth of that and now it's confirmed. Don't tell me. One of Marsha's tricks. Am I right?'

'More than likely.' She was glad he found Marsha amusing. Now that she was no longer here she was beginning to consider her so, too. But dangerous all the same.

'Do you think we should find out what happened to Marsha after Sam and Ginette saw her off, where she went, I mean?' she said.

'Why? Our Marsha is as right as rain with an ankle that has nothing at all wrong with it. I don't know what possessed her to pretend she'd broken it. A lot of people are wondering that.'

Ellie could guess only too well . . . to gain people's sympathy and admiration, her great-aunt's especially, who would provide her with the best accommodation while she pursued Adam. He, of course, would be extra attentive. That Ellie would be ousted from her rooms and Adam's affections was an added bonus.

'I've learned a lot since coming to Cheselton,' Adam said humbly. 'That your pets are guinea pigs, for one. I'm thankful I had the good sense to purchase that lovely oil of Beachy Head you liked before someone else had the same idea. Fool that I was not to realise Marsha's game before.'

190

'But how could you any more than the rest of us? Unless you have particular powers, of course. Maybe that's it.'

Adam's eyes glittered. 'Now you're teasing me.'

'Would I do a thing like that?'

'If you did I'd fully deserve it, Ellie, my dearest love.'

He took a step towards her and she clung to him, feeling his heart beat beneath his jacket as wildly as her own. Then he lowered his head and kissed her.

When he released her he gazed at her with love in his eyes. 'You are beautiful,' he said, his voice husky 'But you're shivering, Ellie. Come, let's feed those animals of yours and get back to the Culmore where we belong before those flimsy sandals sink further into the grass.'

Their arrival was heralded with applause, this time appreciative applause. As Ellie looked round the room she saw Miss Whitlock and her sister, attended by David, taking pride of place near the dais close to the mini orchestra. Ginette and Sam, seemingly unconscious of their surroundings, were seated close together in the corner but looked up as the applause stopped and the music began. Ginette, grinning, did the thumbs-up sign.

As Ellie and Adam began to dance he smelled of fresh air and aftershave. The mix was exotic. For an instant there was clear space on the dance floor and they waltzed into it, the music sweet in her ears. She had never danced like this, never knew that her feet would glide effortlessly with his. It was magic. His hand on the back of her beautiful dress felt strong and confident and she wanted to sing with the wonder of it.

The love in his eyes was nearly her undoing. 'We'll need to think of something else important,' he whispered. 'How about marriage? Would that do for a start, my dearest Eloise?'

'I can't think of anything better,' she murmured.